D0027056

Elizabeth Gaskell

IAP © 2010

Copyright © 2010 by IAP, Las Vegas, Nevada.

admin@iappublishing.com

All rights reserved. This publication is protected by Copyright and written permission should be obtained from the publisher prior to any prohibited reproduction, storage or transmission.

Printed in the US.

Gaskell, Elizabeth.

Lois the Witch / Elizabeth Gaskell– 1st ed.

    1.   Fiction

Contents

Chapter 1   5

Chapter 2   25

Chapter 3   53

Chapter 1

In the year 1691, Lois Barclay stood on a little wooden pier, steadying herself on the stable land, in much the same manner as, eight or nine weeks ago, she had tried to steady herself on the deck of the rocking ship which had carried her across from Old to New England. It seemed as strange now to be on solid earth as it had been, not long ago, to be rocked by the sea both by day and by night; and the aspect of the land was equally strange. The forests which showed in the distance all around, and which, in truth, were not very far from the wooden houses forming the town of Boston, were of different shades of green, and different, too, in shape of outline to those which Lois Barclay knew well in her old home in Warwickshire. Her heart sank a little as she stood alone, waiting for the captain of the good ship Redemption, the kind, rough old sailor, who was her only known friend in this unknown continent. Captain Holdernesse was busy, however, as she saw, and it would probably be some time before he would be ready to attend to her; so Lois sat down on one of the casks that lay about, and wrapped her grey duffle cloak tight around her, and sheltered herself under her hood, as well as might be, from the piercing wind, which seemed to follow those whom it had tyrannized over at sea with a dogged wish of still tormenting them on land. Very patiently did Lois sit there, although she was weary, and shivering with cold; for the day was severe for May, and the Redemption, with store of necessaries and comforts for the Puritan colonists of New England, was the earliest ship that had ventured across the seas.

How could Lois help thinking of the past, and speculating on the future, as she sat on Boston pier, at this breathing-time of her life? In the dim sea mist which she gazed upon with aching eyes (filled, against her will, with tears, from time to time), there rose, the little village church of Barford (not three miles from Warwick--you may see it yet), where her father had preached ever since 1661, long before she was born. He and her mother both lay dead in Barford churchyard; and the old low grey church could hardly come before her vision without her seeing the old parsonage too, the cottage covered with Austrian roses and yellow Jessamine, where she had been born, sole child of parents already long past the prime of youth. She saw the path not a hundred yards long, from the parsonage to the vestry door: that path which her father trod daily; for the vestry was his study, and the sanctum where he pored over the ponderous tomes of the Fathers, and compared their precepts with those of the authorities of the Anglican Church of that day--the day of the later Stuarts; for Barford Parsonage, at that time, scarcely exceeded in size and dignity the cottages by which it was surrounded: it only contained three rooms on a floor, and was but two stories high. On the first or ground floor, were the parlor, kitchen, and back or working kitchen; upstairs, Mr and Mrs Barclay's room, that belonging to Lois, and the maid servant's room. If a guest came, Lois left her own chamber, and shared old Clemence's bed. But those days were over. Never more should Lois see father or mother on earth; they slept, calm and still, in Barford churchyard, careless of what became of their orphan child, as far as earthly manifestations of care or love went. And Clemence lay there too, bound down in her grassy bed by withes of the briar-rose, which Lois had trained over those three precious graves before leaving England for ever.

There were some who would fain have kept her there; one who swore in his heart a great oath unto the Lord that he would seek her, sooner or later, if she was still upon the earth. But he was the rich heir and only son of the Miller Lucy, whose mill stood by the Avon side in the grassy Barford meadows; and his father looked higher for him than the penniless daughter of Parson Barclay (so low were clergymen esteemed in those days!); and the very suspicion of Hugh Lucy's attachment to Lois Barclay made his parents think it more prudent not to offer the orphan a home, although none other of the parishioners had the means, even if they had the will, to do so.

So Lois swallowed her tears down till the time came for crying, and acted upon her mother's words

'Lois, thy father is dead of this terrible fever, and I am dying. Nay, it is so; though I am easier from pain for these few hours, the Lord be praised! The cruel men of the Commonwealth have left thee very friendless. Thy father's only brother was shot down at Edgehill. I, too, have a brother, though thou hast never heard me speak of him, for he was a schismatic; and thy father and me had words, and he left for that new country beyond the seas, without ever saying farewell to us. But Ralph was a kind lad until he took up these newfangled notions; and for the old days sake he will take thee in, and love thee as a child, and place thee among his children. Blood is thicker than water. Write to him as soon as I am gone--for, Lois, I am going, and I bless the Lord that has letten me join my husband again so soon.' Such was the selfishness of conjugal love; she thought little of Lois's desolation in comparison with her rejoicing over her speedy reunion with her dead husband! 'Write to thine uncle, Ralph Hickson, Salem, New England (put it down, child, on thy tablets), and say that I, Henrietta Barclay, charge him, for the sake of all he holds dear in heaven or on earth---for his salvation's sake, as well as for the sake of the old home at Lester Bridge--for the sake of the father and mother that gave us birth, as well as for the sake of the six little children who lie dead between him and me--that he take thee into his home as if thou wert his own flesh and blood, as indeed thou art. He has a wife and children of his own, and no one need fear having thee, my Lois, my darling, my baby, among his household. O Lois, would that thou wert dying with me! The thought of thee makes death sore!' Lois comforted her mother more than herself, poor child, by promises to obey her dying wishes to the letter, and by expressing hopes she dared not feel of her uncle's kindness.

'Promise me'--the dying woman's breath came harder and harder---'that thou wilt go at once. The money our goods will bring--thy letter thy father wrote to Captain Holdernesse, his old schoolfellow--thou knowest all I would say--my Lois, God bless thee!'

Solemnly did Lois promise; strictly she kept her word. It was all the more easy, for Hugh Lucy met her, and told her, in one great burst of love, of his passionate attachment, his vehement struggles with his father, his impotence at present, his hopes and resolves for the future. And, intermingled with all this, came such outrageous threats and expressions of uncontrolled vehemence, that Lois felt that in Barford she must not linger to be a cause of desperate quarrel between father and son, while her absence might soften down matters, so that either the rich old miller might relent, or--and her heart ached to think of the other possibility--Hugh's love might cool, and the dear playfellow of her childhood learn to forget. If not--if Hugh were to be trusted in one tithe of what he said-- God might permit him to fulfill his resolve of coming to seek her out, before many years were over. It was all in God's hands; and that was best, thought Lois Barclay.

She was aroused out of her trance of recollections by Captain Holdernesse, who, having done all that was necessary in the way of orders and directions to his mate, now came up to her, and, praising her for her quiet patience, told her that he would now take her to the Widow Smith's, a decent kind of house, where he and many other sailors of the better order were in the habit of lodging during their stay on the New England shores. Widow Smith, he said, had a parlor for herself and her daughters, in which Lois might sit, while he went about the business that, as he had told her, would detain him in Boston for a day or two, before he could accompany her to her uncle's at Salem. All this had been to a certain degree arranged on ship- board; but Captain Holdernesse, for want of anything else that he could think of to talk about, recapitulated it, as he and Lois walked along. It was his way of showing sympathy with the emotion that made her grey eyes full of tears, as she started up from the pier at the sound of his voice. In his heart he said, 'Poor wench! poor wench! it's a strange land to her, and they are all strange folks, and, I reckon, she will be feeling desolate. I'll try and cheer her up.' So he talked on about hard facts, connected with the life that lay before her, until they reached Widow Smith's; and perhaps Lois was more brightened by this style of conversation, and the new ideas it presented to her, than she would have been by the tenderest woman's sympathy.

'They are a queer set, these New Englanders,' said Captain Holdernesse. 'They are rare chaps for praying; down on their knees at every turn of their life. Folk are none so busy in a new country, else they would have to pray like me, with a "Yo-hoy!" on each side of my prayer, and a rope cutting like fire through my hand. Yon pilot was for calling us all to thanksgiving for a good voyage, and lucky escape from the pirates; but I said I always put up my thanks on dry land, after I had got my ship into harbor. The French colonists, too, are vowing vengeance for the expedition against Canada, and the people here are raging like heathens--at least, as like as godly folk can be--for the loss of their charter. All that is the news the pilot told me; for, for all he wanted us to be thanksgiving instead of casting the lead, he was as down in the mouth as could be about the state of the country. But here we are at Widow Smith's! Now, cheer up, and show the godly a pretty smiling Warwickshire lass!'

Anybody would have smiled at Widow Smith's greeting. She was a comely, motherly woman, dressed in the primmest fashion in vogue twenty years before in England, among the class to which she belonged. But, somehow, her pleasant face gave the lie to her dress; were it as brown and sober-colored as could be, folk remembered it bright and cheerful, because it was a part of Widow Smith herself.

She kissed Lois on both cheeks, before she rightly understood who the stranger maiden was, only because she was a stranger and looked sad and forlorn; and then she kissed her again, because Captain Holdernesse commanded her to the widow's good offices. And so she led Lois by the hand into her rough, substantial log-house, over the door of which hung a great bough of a tree, by way of sign of entertainment for man and horse. Yet not all men were received by Widow Smith. To some she could be as cold and reserved as need be, deaf to all inquiries save one---where else they could find accommodation? To this question she would give a ready answer, and speed the unwelcome guest on his way. Widow Smith was guided in these matters by instinct: one glance at a man's face told her whether or not she chose to have him as an inmate of the same house as her daughters; and her promptness of decision in these matters gave her manner a kind of authority which no one liked to disobey, especially as she had stalwart neighbors within call to back her, if her assumed deafness in the first instance, and her voice and gesture in the second, were not enough to give the would-be guest his dismissal. Widow Smith chose her customers merely by their physical aspect; not one whit with regard to their apparent worldly circumstances. Those who had been staying at her house once always came again; for she had the knack of making every one beneath her roof comfortable and at his ease. Her daughters, Prudence and Hester, had somewhat of their mother's gifts, but not in such perfection. They reasoned a little upon a stranger's appearance, instead of knowing at the first moment whether they liked him or no; they noticed the indications of his clothes, the quality and cut thereof, as telling somewhat of his station in society; they were more reserved; they hesitated more than their mother; they had not her prompt authority, her happy power. Their bread was not so light; their cream went sometimes to sleep, when it should have been turning into butter; their hams were not always just like the hams of the old country'; as their mother's were invariably pronounced to be--yet they were good, orderly, kindly girls, and rose and greeted Lois with a friendly shake of the hand, as their mother, with her arm round the stranger's waist, led her into the private room which she called her parlor. The aspect of this room was strange in the English girl's eyes. The logs of which the house was built showed here and there through the mud-plaster, although before both plaster and logs were hung the skins of many curious animals--skins presented to the widow by many a trader of her acquaintance, just as her sailor-guests brought her another description of gifts--shells, strings of wampum- beads, sea-birds' eggs, and presents from the old country. The room was more like a small museum of natural history of these days than a parlor; and it had a strange, peculiar, but not unpleasant smell about it, neutralized in some degree by the smoke from the enormous trunk of pinewood which smoldered in the hearth.

The instant their mother told them that Captain Holdernesse was in the outer room, the girls began putting away their spinning-wheel and knitting needles, and preparing for a meal of some kind; what meal, Lois, sitting there and unconsciously watching, could hardly tell. First, dough was set to rise for cakes; then came out of a corner- cupboard--a present from England--an enormous square bottle of a cordial called Gold-Wasser; next, a mill for grinding chocolate--a rare, unusual treat anywhere at that time; then a great Cheshire cheese. Three venison-steaks were cut ready for broiling, fat cold pork sliced up and treacle poured over it; a great pie, something like a mince-pie, but which the daughters spoke of with honor as the 'punken-pie,' fresh and salt-fish brandered, oysters cooked in various ways. Lois wondered where would be the end of the provisions for hospitably receiving the strangers from the old country. At length everything was placed on the table, the hot food smoking; but all was cool, not to say cold, before Elder Hawkins (an old neighbor of much repute and standing, who had been invited in by Widow Smith to hear the news) had finished his grace, into which was embodied thanksgiving for the past, and prayers for the future, lives of every individual present, adapted to their several cases, as far as the elder could guess at them from appearances. This grace might not have ended so soon as it did, had it not been for the somewhat impatient drumming of his knife-handle on the table, with which Captain

Holdernesse accompanied the latter half of the elder's words.

When they first sat down to their meal, all were too hungry for much talking; but, as their appetites diminished, their curiosity increased, and there was much to be told and heard on both sides. With all the English intelligence Lois was, of course, well acquainted; but she listened with natural attention to all that was said about the new country, and the new people among whom she had come to live. Her father had been a Jacobite, as the adherents of the Stuarts were beginning at this rime to be called. His father, again, had been a follower of Archbishop Laud; so Lois had hitherto heard little of the conversation, and seen little of the ways of the Puritans. Elder Hawkins was one of the strictest of the strict, and evidently his presence kept the two daughters of the house considerably in awe. But the widow herself was a privileged person; her known goodness of heart (the effects of which had been experienced by many) gave her the liberty of speech which was tacitly denied to many, under penalty of being esteemed ungodly, if they infringed certain conventional limits. And Captain Holdernesse and his mate spoke out their minds, let who would be present. So that, on this first landing in New England, Lois was, as it were, gently let down into the midst of the Puritan peculiarities; and yet they were sufficient to make her feel very lonely and strange.

The first subject of conversation was the present state of the colony--Lois soon found out that, although at the beginning she was not a little perplexed by the frequent reference to names of places which she naturally associated with the old country. Widow Smith was speaking: 'In county of Essex the folk are ordered to keep four scouts, or companies of minutemen; six persons in each company; to be on the look-out for the wild Indians, who are for ever stirring about in the woods, stealthy brutes as they are! I am sure, I got such a fright the first harvest-time after I came over to New England, I go on dreaming, now near twenty years after Lothrop's business, of painted Indians, with their shaven scalps and their war-streaks, lurking behind the trees, and coming nearer and nearer with their noiseless steps.'

Yes,' broke in one of her daughters; 'and, mother, don't you remember how Hannah Benson told us how her husband had cut down every tree near his house at Deerbrook, in order that no one might come near him, under cover;

and how one evening she was a-sitting in the twilight, when all her family were gone to bed, and her husband gone off to Plymouth on business, and she saw a log of wood, just like a trunk of a felled tree, lying in the shadow, and thought nothing of it, till, on looking again a while after, she fancied it was come a bit nearer to the house; and how her heart turned sick with fright; and how she dared not stir at first, but shut her eyes while she counted a hundred, and looked again, and the shadow was deeper, but she could see that the log was nearer; so she ran in and bolted the door, and went up to where her eldest lad lay. It was Elijah, and he was but sixteen then; but he rose up at his mother's words, and took his father's long duck-gun down; and he tried the loading, and spoke for the first time to put up a prayer that God would give his aim good guidance, and went to a window that gave a view upon the side where the log lay, and fired; and no one dared to look what came of it; but all the household read the Scriptures, and prayed the whole night long; till morning came and showed a long stream of blood lying on the grass close by the log---which the full sunlight showed to be no log at all, but just a Red Indian covered with bark, and painted most skillfully, with his war-knife by his side.'

All were breathless with listening; though to most the story, or others like it, were familiar. Then another took up the tale of horror:--

'And the pirates have been down at Marblehead, since you were here, Captain Holdernesse. 'Twas only the last winter they landed--French Papist pirates; and the people kept close within their houses, for they knew not what would come of it; and they dragged folk ashore. There was one woman among those folk-- prisoners from some vessel, doubtless---and the pirates took them by force to the inland marsh; and the Marblehead folk kept still and quiet, every gun loaded, and every car on the watch, for who knew but what the wild sea-robbers might take a turn on land next; and, in the dead of the night, they heard a woman's loud and pitiful outcry from the marsh, "Lord Jesu! have mercy on me! Save me from the power of man, O Lord Jesu!" And the blood of all who heard the cry ran cold with terror; till old Nance Hickson, who had been stone-deaf and bed-ridden for years, stood up in the midst of the folk all gathered together in her grandson's house, and said, that, as they, the dwellers in Marblehead, had not had brave hearts or faith enough to go and succor the helpless, that cry of a dying woman should be in their ears, and in their children's cars, till the end of the world. And Nance dropped down dead as soon as she had made an end of speaking, and the pirates set sail from Marblehead at morning dawn; but the folk there hear the cry still, shrill and pitiful, from the waste marshes, "Lord Jesu! have mercy on me! Save me from the power of man, O Lord Jesu!"'

'And, by token,' said Elder Hawkins's deep bass voice, speaking with the strong nasal twang of the Puritans (who, says Butler, 'godly Mr Noyes ordained a fast at Marblehead, and preached a soul-stirring discourse on the words, "Inasmuch as ye did it not unto one of the least of these, my brethren, ye did it not unto me." But it has been borne in upon me at times, whether the whole vision of the pirates and the cry of the woman was not a device of Satan's to sift the Marblehead folk, and see what fruit their doctrine bore, and so to condemn them in the sight of the Lord. If it were so, the enemy had a great triumph; for assuredly it was no part of Christian men to leave a helpless woman unaided in her sore distress.)'

'But, Elder,' said Widow Smith, 'it was no vision; they were real living men who went ashore, men who broke down branches and left their footmarks on the ground.'

'As for that matter, Satan hath many powers, and, if it be the day when he is permitted to go about like a roaring lion, he will not stick at trifles, but make his work complete. I tell you, many men are spiritual enemies in visible forms, permitted to roam about the waste places of the earth. I myself believe that these Red Indians are indeed the evil creatures of whom we read in Holy Scripture; and there is no doubt that they are in league with those abominable Papists, the French people in Canada. I have heard tell, that the French pay the Indians so much gold for every dozen scalps of Englishmen's heads.'

'Pretty cheerful talk this!' said Captain Holdernesse to Lois, perceiving her blanched cheek and terror-stricken mien. 'Thou art thinking that thou hadst better have stayed at Barford, I'll answer for it, wench. But the devil is not so black as he is painted.'

'Ho! there again!' said Elder Hawkins. 'The devil is painted, it hath been said so from old times; and are not these Indians painted, even like unto their father?'

'But is it all true?' asked Lois, aside, of Captain Holdernesse, letting the Elder hold forth unheeded by her, though listened to with the utmost reverence by the two daughters of the house.

'My wench,' said the old sailor, 'thou hast come to a country where there are many perils, both from land and from sea. The Indians hate the white men. Whether other white men' (meaning the French away to the north) 'have bounded-on the savages, or whether the English have taken their lands and hunting-grounds without due recompense, and so raised the cruel vengeance of the wild creatures--who knows? But it is true that it is not safe to go far into the woods, for fear of the lurking painted savages; nor has it been safe to build a dwelling far from a settlement; and it takes a brave heart to make a journey from one town to another; and folk do say the Indian creatures rise up out of the very ground to waylay the English! and then others affirm they are all in league with Satan to affright the Christians out of the heathen country, over which he has reigned so long. Then, again, the sea-shore is infested by pirates, the scum of all nations: they land, and plunder, and ravage, and burn, and destroy. Folk get affrighted of the real dangers, and in their fright imagine, perchance, dangers that are not. But who knows? Holy Scripture speaks of witches and wizards, and of the power of the Evil One in desert places; and, even in the old country, we have heard tell of those who have sold their souls for ever for the little power they get for a few years on earth.'

By this time the whole table was silent, listening to the captain; it was just one of those chance silences that sometimes occur, without any apparent reason, and often without any apparent consequence. But all present had reason, before many months had passed over, to remember the words which Lois spoke in answer, although her voice was low, and she only thought, in the interest of the moment, of being heard by her old friend the captain.

'They are fearful creatures, the witches! and yet I am sorry for the poor old women, whilst I dread them. We had one in Barford, when I was a little child. No one knew whence she came, but she settled herself down in a mud-hut by the common-side; and there she lived, she and her cat.' (At the mention of the cat, Elder Hawkins shook his head long and gloomily.) 'No one knew how she lived, if it were not on nettles and scraps of oatmeal and such-like food, given her more for fear than for pity. She went double, and always talking and muttering to herself. Folk said she snared birds and rabbits in the thicket that came down to her hovel. How it came to pass I cannot say, but many a one fell sick in the village, and much cattle died one spring, when I was near four years old. I never heard much about it, for my father said it was ill talking about such things; I only know I got a sick fright one afternoon, when the maid had gone out for milk and had taken me with her, and we were passing a meadow where the Avon, circling, makes a deep round pool, and there was a crowd of folk, all still--and a still, breathless crowd makes the heart beat worse than a shouting, noisy one. They were all gazing towards the water, and the maid held me up in her arms, to see the sight above the shoulders of the people; and I saw old Hannah in the water, her grey hair all streaming down her shoulders, and her face bloody and black with the stones and mud they had been throwing at her, and her cat tied round her neck. I hid my face, I know, as soon as I saw the fearsome sight, for her eyes met mine as they were glaring with fury--poor, helpless, baited creature!--and she caught the sight of me, and cried out, "Parson's wench, parson's wench, yonder, in thy nurse's arms, thy dad bath never tried for to save me; and none shall save thee, when thou art brought up for a witch." Oh! the words rang in my cars, when I was dropping asleep, for years after. I used to dream that I was in that pond; that all men hated me with their eyes because I was a witch: and, at times, her black cat used to seem living again, and say over those dreadful works.'

Lois stopped: the two daughters looked at her excitement with a kind of shrinking surprise, for the tears were in her eyes. Elder Hawkins shook his head, and muttered texts from Scripture; but cheerful Widow Smith, not liking the gloomy rum of the conversation, tried to give it a lighter cast by saying, 'And I don't doubt but what the parson's bonny lass has bewitched many a one since, with her dimples and her pleasant ways--eh, Captain Holdernesse? It's you must tell us tales of the young lass's doings in England.'

'Ay, ay,' said the captain; 'there's one under her charms in Warwickshire who will never get the better of it, I'm thinking.'

Elder Hawkins rose to speak; he stood leaning on his hands, which were placed on the table: 'Brethren,' said he, 'I must upbraid you if ye speak lightly; charms and witchcraft are evil things; I trust this maiden bath had nothing to do with them, even in thought. But my mind misgives me at her story. The hellish witch might have power from Satan to infect her mind, she being yet a child, with the deadly sin. Instead of vain talking, I call upon you all to join with me in prayer for this stranger in our land, that her heart may be purged from all iniquity. Let us pray.'

'Come, there's no harm in that,' said the captain; 'but, Elder Hawkins, when you are at work, just pray for us all; for I am afeard there be some of us need purging from iniquity a good deal more than Lois Barclay, and a prayer for a man never does mischief.'

Captain Holdernesse had business in Boston which detained him there for a couple of days; and during that time Lois remained with the Widow Smith, seeing what was to be seen of the new land that contained her future home. The letter of her dying mother was sent off to Salem, meanwhile, by a lad going thither, in order to prepare her Uncle Ralph Hickson for his niece's coming, as soon as Captain Holdernesse could find leisure to take her; for he considered her given into his own personal charge, until he could consign her to her uncle's care. When the time came for going to Salem, Lois felt very sad at leaving the kindly woman under whose roof she had been staying, and looked back as long as she could see anything of Widow Smith's dwelling. She was packed into a rough kind of country-cart, which just held her and Captain Holdernesse, beside the driver. There was a basket of provisions under their feet, and behind them hung a bag of provender for the horse; for it was a good day's journey to Salem, and the road was reputed so dangerous that it was ill tarrying a minute longer than necessary for refreshment. English roads were bad enough at that period, and for long after; but in America the way was simply the cleared ground of the forest--the stumps of the felled trees still remaining in the direct line, forming obstacles which it required the most careful driving to avoid; and in the hollows, where the ground was swampy, the pulpy nature of it was obviated by logs of wood laid across the boggy part. The deep green forest, tangled into heavy darkness even thus early in the year, came within a few yards of the road all the way, though efforts were regularly made by the inhabitants of the neighboring settlements to keep a certain space clear on each side, for fear of the lurking Indians, who might otherwise come upon them unawares. The cries of strange birds, the unwonted color of some of them, all suggested to the imaginative or unaccustomed traveler the idea of war-whoops and painted deadly enemies. But at last they drew near to Salem, which rivaled Boston in size in those days, and boasted the names of one or two streets, although to an English eye they looked rather more like irregularly built houses, clustered round the meeting-house, or rather one of the meeting-houses, for a second was in process of building. The whole place was surrounded with two circles of stockades; between the two were the gardens and grazing-ground for those who dreaded their cattle straying into the woods, and the consequent danger of reclaiming them.

The lad who drove them flogged his spent horse into a trot, as they went through Salem to Ralph Hickson's house. It was evening, the leisure-time for the inhabitants, and their children were at play before the houses. Lois was struck by the beauty of one wee, toddling child, and turned to look after it; it caught its little foot in a stump of wood, and fell with a cry that brought the mother out in affright. As she ran out, her eye caught Lois' anxious gaze, although the noise of the heavy wheels drowned the sound of her words of inquiry as to the nature of the hurt the child had received. Nor had Lois time to think long upon the matter; for, the instant after, the horse was pulled up at the door of a good, square, substantial wooden house, plastered over into a creamy white, perhaps as handsome a house as any in Salem; and there she was told by the driver that her uncle, Ralph Hickson, lived. In the flurry of the moment she did not notice, but Captain Holdernesse did, that no one came out at the unwonted sound of wheels, to receive and welcome her. She was lifted down by the old sailor, and led into a large room, almost like the hall of some English manor-house as to size. A tall, gaunt young man of three or four-and-twenty sat on a bench by one of the windows, reading a great folio by the fading light of day. He did not rise when they came in, but looked at them with surprise, no gleam of intelligence coming into his stem, dark face. There was no woman in the house-place. Captain Holdernesse paused a moment, and then said--

'Is this house Ralph Hickson's?'

'It is,' said the young man, in a slow, deep voice. But he added no word further.

'This is his niece, Lois Barclay,' said the captain, taking the girl's arm, and pushing her forwards. The young man looked at her steadily and gravely for a minute; then rose, and carefully marking the page in the folio, which hitherto had laid open upon his knee, said, still in the same heavy, indifferent manner, 'I will call my mother; she will know.'

He opened a door which looked into a warm bright kitchen, ruddy with the light of the fire, over which three women were apparently engaged in cooking something, while a fourth, an old Indian woman, of a greenish-brown color, shriveled-up and bent with apparent age, moved backwards and forwards, evidently fetching the others the articles they required.

'Mother!' said the young man; and, having arrested her attention, he pointed over his shoulder to the newly-arrived strangers and returned to the study of his book, from time to time, however, furtively examining Lois from beneath his dark shaggy eyebrows.

A tall, largely-made woman, past middle life, came in from the kitchen, and stood reconnoitring the strangers.

Captain Holdernesse spoke--

'This is Lois Barclay, master Ralph Hickson's niece.'

'I know nothing of her,' said the mistress of the house in a deep voice, almost as masculine as her son's.

'Master Hickson received his sister's letter, did he not? I sent it off myself by a lad named Elias Wellcome, who left Boston for this place yester morning.'

'Ralph Hickson has received no such letter. He lies bed-ridden in the chamber beyond. Any letters for him must come through my hands; wherefore I can affirm with certainty that no such letter has been delivered here. His sister Barclay, she that was Henrietta Hickson, and whose husband took the oaths to

Charles Stuart, and stuck by his living when all godly men left theirs'--

Lois, who had thought her heart was dead and cold, a minute before, at the ungracious reception she had met with, felt words come up into her mouth at the implied insult to her father, and spoke out, to her own and the captain's astonishment--

'They might be godly men who left their churches on that day of which you speak, madam; but they alone were not the godly men, and no one has a right to limit true godliness for mere opinion's sake.'

'Well said, lass,' spoke out the captain, looking round upon her with a kind of admiring wonder, and patting her on the back.

Lois and her aunt gazed into each other's eyes unflinchingly, for a minute or two of silence; but the girl felt her color coming and going, while the elder woman's never varied; and the eyes of the young maiden were filling fast with tears, while those of Grace Hickson kept on their stare, dry and unwavering.

'Mother,' said the young man, rising up with a quicker motion than any one had yet used in this house, 'it is ill speaking of such matters when my cousin comes first among us. The Lord may give her grace hereafter; but she has travelled from Boston city today, and she and this seafaring man must need rest and food.'

He did not attend to see the effect of his words, but sat down again, and seemed to be absorbed in his book in an instant. Perhaps he knew that his word was law with his grim mother; for he had hardly ceased speaking before she had pointed to a wooden settle; and, smoothing the lines on her countenance, she said-- 'What Manasseh says is true. Sit down here, while I bid Faith and Nattee get food ready; and meanwhile I will go tell my husband that one who calls herself his sister's child is come over to pay him a visit.'

She went to the door leading into the kitchen, and gave some directions to the elder girl, whom Lois now knew to be the daughter of the house. Faith stood impassive, while her mother spoke, scarcely caring to look at the newly-arrived strangers. She was like her brother Manasseh in complexion, but had handsomer features, and large, mysterious-looking eyes, as Lois saw, when once she lifted them up, and took in, as it were, the aspect of the sea-captain and her cousin with one swift, searching look. About the stiff, tall, angular mother, and the scarce less pliant figure of the daughter, a girl of twelve years old, or thereabouts, played all manner of impish antics, unheeded by them, as if it were her accustomed habit to peep about, now under their arms, now at this side, now at that, making grimaces all the while at Lois and Captain Holdernesse, who sat facing the door, weary, and somewhat disheartened by their reception. The captain pulled out tobacco, and began to chew it by way of consolation; but in a moment or two his usual elasticity of spirit came to his rescue, and he said in a low voice to Lois--

'That scoundrel Elias, I will give it him! If the letter had but been delivered, thou wouldst have had a different kind of welcome; but, as soon as I have had some victuals, I will go out and find the lad, and bring back the letter, and that will make all right, my wench. Nay, don't be down-hearted, for I cannot stand women's tears. Thou'rt just worn out with the shaking and the want of food.'

Lois brushed away her tears, and, looking round to try and divert her thoughts by fixing them on present objects, she caught her cousin Manasseh's deep-set eyes furtively watching her. It was with no unfriendly gaze; yet it made Lois uncomfortable, particularly as he did not withdraw his looks, after he must have seen that she observed him. She was glad when her aunt called her into an inner room to see her uncle, and she escaped from the steady observance of her gloomy, silent cousin.

Ralph Hickson was much older than his wife, and his illness made him look older still. He had never had the force of character that Grace, his spouse, possessed; and age and sickness had now rendered him almost childish at times. But his nature was affectionate; and, stretching out his trembling arms from whence he lay bedridden, he gave Lois an unhesitating welcome, never waiting for the confirmation of the missing letter before he acknowledged her to be his niece.

'Oh! 'tis kind in thee to come all across the sea to make acquaintance with thine uncle; kind in sister Barclay to spare thee!'

Lois had to tell him, there was no one living to miss her at home in England; that, in fact, she had no home in England, no father nor mother left upon earth; and that she had been bidden by her mother's last words to seek him out and ask him for a home. Her words came up, half choked from a heavy heart, and his dulled wits could not take in their meaning without several repetitions; and then he cried like a child, rather at his own loss of a sister whom he had not seen for more than twenty years, than at that of the orphan's, standing before him, trying hard not to cry, but to start bravely in this new strange home. What most of all helped Lois in her self-restraint was her aunt's unsympathetic look. Born and bred in New England, Grace Hickson had a kind of jealous dislike to her husband's English relations, which had increased since of late years his weakened mind yearned after them; and he forgot the good reason he had had for his self- exile, and moaned over the decision which had led to it as the great mistake of his life. 'Come,' said she; 'it strikes me that, in all this sorrow for the loss of one who died full of years, ye are forgetting in Whose hands life and death are!'

True words, but ill-spoken at that time. Lois looked up at her with a scarcely disguised indignation; which increased as she heard the contemptuous tone in which her aunt went on talking to Ralph Hickson, even while she was arranging his bed with a regard to his greater comfort.

'One would think thou wert a godless man, by the moan thou art always making over spilt milk; and truth is, thou art but childish in thine old age. When we were wed, thou left all things to the Lord; I would never have married thee else. Nay, lass,' said she, catching the expression on Lois's face, 'thou art never going to browbeat me with thine angry looks. I do my duty as I read it, and there is never a man in Salem that dare speak a word to Grace Hickson about either her works or her faith. Godly Mr Cotton Mather bath said, that even he might learn of me; and I would advise thee rather to humble thyself, and see if the Lord may not convert thee from thy ways, since He has sent thee to dwell, as it were, in Zion, where the precious dew fails daily on Aaron's beard.'

Lois felt ashamed and sorry to find that her aunt had so truly interpreted the momentary expression of her features; she blamed herself a little for the feeling that had caused that expression, trying to think how much her aunt might have been troubled with something, before the unexpected irruption of the strangers, and again hoping that the remembrance of this misunderstanding would soon pass away. So she endeavored to reassure herself, and not to give way to her uncle's tender trembling pressure of her hand, as, at her aunt's bidding, she wished him 'goodnight', and returned into the outer, or 'keeping'-- room, where all the family were now assembled, ready for the meal of flourcakes and venison steaks which Nattee, the Indian servant, was bringing in from the kitchen. No one seemed to have been speaking to Captain Holdernesse, while Lois had been away. Manasseh sat quiet and silent where he did, with the book open upon his knee; his eyes thoughtfully fixed on vacancy, as if he saw a vision, or dreamed dreams. Faith stood by the table, lazily directing Nattee in her preparations; and Prudence lofted against the door-frame, between kitchen and keeping-room, playing tricks on the old Indian woman, as she passed backwards and forwards, till Nattee appeared to be in a state of strong irritation, which she tried in vain to suppress; as, whenever she showed any sign of it, Prudence only seemed excited to greater mischief. When all was ready, Manasseh lifted his right hand and 'asked a blessing,' as it was termed; but the grace became a long prayer for abstract spiritual blessings, for strength to combat Satan, and to quench his fiery darts, and at length assumed-- so Lois thought--a purely personal character, as if the young man had forgotten the occasion, and even the people present, but was searching into the nature of the diseases that beset his own sick soul, and spreading them out before the Lord. He was brought back by a pluck at the coat from Prudence; he opened his shut eyes, cast an angry glance at the child, who made a face at him for sole reply, and then he sat down, and they all fell to. Grace Hickson would have thought her hospitality sadly at fault, if she had allowed Captain Holdernesse to go out in search of a bed. Skins were spread for him on the floor of the keeping-room; a Bible and a square bottle of spirits were placed on the table to supply his wants during the night; and, in spite of all the cares and troubles, temptations, or sins of the members of that household, they were all asleep before the town clock struck ten.

In the morning, the captain's first care was to go out in search of the boy Elias and the missing letter. He met him bringing it with an easy conscience, for, thought Elias, a few hours sooner or later will make no difference; tonight or the morrow morning will be all the same. But he was startled into a sense of wrong-doing, by a sound box on the ear from the very man who had charged him to deliver it speedily, and whom he believed to be at that very moment in Boston city.

The letter delivered, all possible proof being given that Lois had a right to claim a home from her nearest relations, Captain Holdernesse thought it best to take leave.

'Thou'lt take to them, lass, maybe, when there is no one here to make thee think on the old country. Nay, nay! parting is hard work at all times, and best get hard work done out of hand! Keep up thine heart, my wench, and I'll come back and see thee next spring, if we are all spared till then; and who knows what fine young miller mayn't come with me? Don't go and get wed to a praying Puritan, meanwhile! There, there; I'm off. God bless thee!'

And Lois was left alone in New England.

Chapter 3

It was hard work for Lois to win herself a place in this family. Her aunt was a woman of narrow, strong affections. Her love for her husband, if ever she had any, was burnt out and dead long ago. What she did for him, she did from duty; but duty was not strong enough to restrain that little member, the tongue; and Lois's heart often bled at the continual flow of contemptuous reproof which Grace constantly addressed to her husband, even while she was sparing no pains or trouble to minister to his bodily case and comfort. It was more as a relief to herself that she spoke in this way, than with any desire that her speeches should affect him; and he was too deadened by illness to feel hurt by them; or, it may be, the constant repetition of her sarcasms had made him indifferent; at any rate, so that he had his food and his state of bodily warmth attended to, he very seldom seemed to care much for anything else. Even his first flow of affection towards Lois was soon exhausted; he cared for her, because she arranged his pillows well and skillfully, and because she could prepare new and dainty kinds of food for his sick appetite, but no longer for her as his dead sister's child. Still he did care for her, and Lois was too glad of his little hoard of affection to examine how or why it was given. To him she could give pleasure, but apparently to no one else in that household. Her aunt looked askance at her for many reasons: the first coming of Lois to Salem was inopportune; the expression of disapprobation on her face on that evening still lingered and rankled in Grace's memory; early prejudices, and feelings, and prepossessions of the English girl were all on the side of what would now be called Church and State, what was then esteemed in that country a superstitious observance of the directions of a Popish rubric, and a servile regard for the family of an oppressing and irreligious king. Nor is it to be supposed that Lois did not feel, and feel acutely, the want of sympathy that all those with whom she was now living manifested towards the old hereditary loyalty (religious as well as political loyalty) in which she had been brought up. With her aunt and Manasseh it was more than want of sympathy; it was positive, active antipathy to all the ideas Lois held most dear. The very allusion, however incidentally made, to the little old grey church at Barford, where her father had preached so long--the occasional reference to the troubles in which her own country had been distracted when she left--and the adherence, in which she had been brought up, to the notion that the king could do no wrong, seemed to irritate Manasseh past endurance. He would get up from his reading, his constant employment when at home, and walk angrily about the room after Lois had said anything of this kind, muttering to himself; and once he had even stopped before her, and in a passionate tone bade her not talk so like a fool. Now this was very different to his mother's sarcastic, contemptuous way of treating all poor Lois's little loyal speeches. Grace would lead her on--at least she did at first, till experience made Lois wiser--to express her thoughts on such subjects, till, just when the girl's heart was opening, her aunt would turn round upon her with some bitter sneer that roused all the evil feelings in Lois's disposition by its sting. Now Manasseh seemed, through all his anger, to be so really grieved by what he considered her error, that he went much nearer to convincing her that there might be two sides to a question. Only this was a view that it appeared like treachery to her dead father's memory to entertain.

Somehow, Lois felt instinctively that Manasseh was really friendly towards her. He was little in the house; there was farming, and some kind of mercantile business to be transacted by him, as real head of the house; and, as the season drew on, he went shooting and hunting in the surrounding forests, with a daring which caused his mother to warn and reprove him in private, although to the neighbors she boasted largely of her son's courage and disregard of danger. Lois did not often walk out for the mere sake of walking; there was generally some household errand to be transacted when any of the women of the family went abroad; but once or twice she had caught glimpses of the dreary, dark wood, hemming in the cleared land on all sides--the great wood with its perpetual movement of branch and bough, and its solemn wail, that came into the very streets of Salem when certain winds blew, bearing the sound of the pine-trees clear upon the ears that had leisure to listen. And, from all accounts, this old forest, girdling round the settlement, was full of dreaded and mysterious beasts, and still more to be dreaded Indians, stealing in and out among the shadows, intent on bloody schemes against the Christian people:

panther-streaked, shaven Indians, in league by their own confession, as well as by the popular belief, with evil powers.

Nattee, the old Indian servant, would occasionally make Lois's blood run cold, as she and Faith and Prudence listened to the wild stories she told them of the wizards of her race. It was often in the kitchen, in the darkening evening, while some cooking process was going on, that the old Indian crone, sitting on her haunches by the bright red wood embers which sent up no flame, but a lurid light reversing the shadows of all the faces around, told her weird stories, while they were awaiting the rising of the dough, perchance, out of which the household bread had to be made. There ran through these stories always a ghastly, unexpressed suggestion of some human sacrifice being needed to complete the success of any incantation to the Evil One; and the poor old creature, herself believing and shuddering as she narrated her tale in broken English, took a strange, unconscious pleasure in her power over her hearers-- young girls of the oppressing race, which had brought her down into a state little differing from slavery, and reduced her people to outcasts on the hunting-grounds which had belonged to her fathers.

After such tales, it required no small effort on Lois's part to go out, at her aunt's command, into the common pasture round the town, and bring the cattle home at night. Who knew but what the double- headed snake might start up from each blackberry bush--that wicked, cunning, accursed creature in the service of the Indian wizards, that had such power over all those white maidens who met the eyes placed at either end of his long, sinuous, creeping body, so that, loathe him, loathe the Indian race as they would, off they must go into the forest to seek out some Indian man, and must beg to be taken into his wigwam, adjuring faith and race for ever? Or there were spells--so Nattee said--hidden about the ground by the wizards, which changed that person's nature who found them; so that, gentle and loving as they might have been before, thereafter they took no pleasure but in the cruel torments of others, and had a strange power given to them of causing such torments at their will. Once, Nattee, speaking low to Lois, who was alone with her in the kitchen, whispered out her terrified belief that such a spell had Prudence found; and, when the Indian showed her arms to Lois, all pinched black and blue by the impish child, the English girl began to be afraid of her cousin as of one possessed. But it was not Nattee alone, nor young imaginative girls alone, that believed in these stories. We can afford to smile at them now; but our English ancestors entertained superstitions of much the same character at the same period, and with less excuse, as the circumstances surrounding them were better known, and consequently more explicable by common sense, than the real mysteries of the deep, untrodden forests of New England. The gravest divines not only believed stories similar to that of the double-headed serpent, and other tales of witchcraft, but they made such narrations the subjects of preaching and prayer; and, as cowardice makes us all cruel, men who were blameless in many of the relations of life, and even praiseworthy in some, became, from superstition, cruel persecutors about this time, showing no mercy towards any one whom they believed to be in league with the Evil One.

Faith was the person with whom the English girl was the most intimately associated in her uncle's house. The two were about the same age, and certain household employments were shared between them. They took it in turns to call in the cows, to make up the butter which had been churned by Hosea, a stiff, old out-door servant, in whom Grace Hickson placed great confidence; and each lassie had her great spinning-wheel for wool, and her lesser for flax, before a month had elapsed after Lois's coming. Faith was a grave, silent person, never merry, sometimes very sad, though Lois was a long time in even guessing why. She would try, in her sweet, simple fashion, to cheer her cousin up, when the latter was depressed, by telling her old stories of English ways and life. Occasionally, Faith seemed to care to listen; occasionally, she did not heed one word, but dreamed on. Whether of the past or of the future, who could tell?

Stern old ministers came in to pay their pastoral visits. On such occasions, Grace Hickson would put on clean apron and clean cap, and make them more welcome than she was ever seen to do any one else, bringing out the best provisions of her store, and setting of all before them. Also, the great Bible was brought forth, and Hosea and Nattee summoned from their work, to listen while the minister read a chapter, and, as he read, expounded it at considerable length. After this all knelt, while he, standing, lifted up his right hand, and prayed for all possible combinations of Christian men, for all possible cases of spiritual need; and lastly, taking the individuals before him, he would put up a very personal supplication for each, according to his notion of their wants. At first,

Lots wondered at the aptitude of one or two of his prayers of this description to the outward circumstances of each case; but, when she perceived that her aunt had usually a pretty long confidential conversation with the minister in the early part of his visit, she became aware that he received both his impressions and his knowledge through the medium of 'that godly woman, Grace Hickson;' and I am afraid she paid less regard to the prayer 'for the maiden from another land, who bath brought the errors of that land as a seed with her, even across the great ocean, and who is letting even now the little seeds shoot up into an evil tree, in which all unclean creatures may find shelter.'

'I like the prayers of our Church better,' said Lois one day to Faith. 'No clergyman in England can pray his own words; and therefore it is that he does not judge of others so as to fit his prayers to what he esteems to be their case, as Mr Tappau did this morning.'

'I hate Mr Tappau!' said Faith shortly, a passionate flash of light coming out of her dark, heavy eyes.

'Why so, cousin? It seems to me as if he were a good man, although I like not his prayers.'

Faith only repeated her words, 'I hate him!'

Lois was sorry for this strong, bad feeling; instinctively sorry, for she was loving herself, delighted in being loved, and felt a jar run through her at every sign of want of love in others. But she did not know what to say, and was silent at the time. Faith, too, went on turning her wheel with vehemence, but spoke never a word until her thread snapped; and then she pushed the wheel away hastily, and left the room.

Then Prudence crept softly up to Lois's side. This strange child seemed to be tossed about by varying moods: today she was caressing and communicative; tomorrow she might be deceitful, mocking, and so indifferent to the pain or sorrows of others that you could call her almost inhuman.

'So thou dost not like Pastor Tappau's prayers?' she whispered.

Lots was sorry to have been overheard; but she neither would nor could take back her words.

'I like them not so well as the prayers I used to hear at home.'

'Mother says thy home was with the ungodly. Nay, don't look at me so-- it was not I that said it. I'm none so fond of praying myself, nor of Pastor Tappau, for that matter. But Faith cannot abide him, and I know why. Shall I tell thee, Cousin Lois?'

'No! Faith did not tell me; and she was the right person to give her own reasons.'

'Ask her where young Mr Nolan is gone to, and thou wilt hear. I have seen Faith cry by the hour together about Mr Nolan.'

'Hush, child! hush!' said Lois, for she heard Faith's approaching step, and feared lest she should overhear what they were saying.

The truth was that, a year or two before, there had been a great struggle in Salem village, a great division in the religious body, and Pastor Tappau had been the leader of the more violent, and, ultimately, the successful party. In consequence of this, the less popular minister, Mr Nolan, had had to leave the place. And him Faith Hickson loved with all the strength of her passionate heart, although he never was aware of the attachment he had excited, and her own family were too regardless of manifestations of mere feeling ever to observe the signs of any emotion on her part. But the old Indian servant Nattee saw and observed them all. She knew, as well as if she had been told the reason, why Faith had lost all care about father or mother, brother and sister, about household work and daily occupation; nay, about the observances of religion as well. Nattee read the meaning of the deep smoldering of Faith's dislike to Pastor Tappau aright; the Indian woman understood why the girl (whom alone of all the white people she loved) avoided the old minister--would hide in the wood-stack, sooner than be called in to listen to his exhortations and prayers. With savage, untutored people, it is not 'Love me, love my dog,'--they are often jealous of the creature beloved; but it is, 'Whom thou hatest I will hate;' and Nattee's feeling towards Pastor Tappau was even an exaggeration of the mute, unspoken hatred of Faith.

For a long time, the cause of her cousin's dislike and avoidance of the minister was a mystery to Lois; but the name of Nolan remained in her memory, whether she would or no; and it was more from girlish interest in a suspected love affair, than from any indifferent and heartless curiosity, that she could not help piecing together little speeches and actions with Faith's interest in the absent banished minister, for an explanatory clue, till not a doubt remained in her mind. And this without any further communication with Prudence, for Lois declined hearing any more on the subject from her, and so gave deep offence.

Faith grew sadder and duller, as the autumn drew on. She lost her appetite; her brown complexion became sallow and colorless; her dark eyes looked hollow and wild. The first of November was near at hand. Lois, in her instinctive, well-intentioned efforts to bring some life and cheerfulness into the monotonous household, had been telling Faith of many English customs, silly enough, no doubt, and which scarcely lighted up a flicker of interest in the American girl's mind. The cousins were lying awake in their bed, in the great unplastered room, which was in part storeroom, in part bedroom. Lois was full of sympathy for Faith that night. For long she had listened to her cousin's heavy, irrepressible sighs, in silence. Faith sighed, because her grief was of too old a date for violent emotion or crying. Lois listened without speaking in the dark, quiet night hours, for a long, long time. She kept quite still, because she thought such vent for sorrow might relieve her cousin's weary heart. But, when at length, instead of lying motionless, Faith seemed to be growing restless, even to convulsive motions of her limbs, Lois began to speak, to talk about England, and the dear old ways at home, without exciting much attention on Faith's part; until at length she fell upon the subject of Hallow-e'en, and told about customs then and long afterwards practiced in England, and that have scarcely yet died out in Scotland. As she told of tricks she had often played, of the apple eaten facing a mirror, of the dripping sheet, of the basins of water, of the nuts burning side by side, and many other such innocent ways of divination, by which laughing, trembling English maidens sought to see the form of their future husbands, if husbands they were to have: then Faith listened breathlessly, asking short eager questions, as if some ray of hope had entered into her gloomy heart. Lois went on speaking, telling her of all the stories that would confirm the truth of the second sight vouchsafed to all seekers in the accustomed methods; half believing, half incredulous herself, but desiring, above all things, to cheer up poor Faith.

Suddenly, Prudence rose up from her truckle-bed in the dim corner of the room. They had not thought that she was awake; but she had been listening long.

'Cousin Lois may go out and meet Satan by the brookside, if she will; but, if thou goest, Faith, I will tell mother--ay, and I will tell Pastor Tappau, too. Hold thy stories, Cousin Lois; I am afeared of my very life. I would rather never be wed at all, than feel the touch of the creature that would take the apple out of my hand, as I held it over my left shoulder.' The excited girl gave a loud scream of terror at the image her fancy had conjured up. Faith and Lois sprang out towards her, flying across the moon-lit room in their white night-gowns. At the same instant, summoned by the same cry, Grace Hickson came to her child.

'Hush! hush!' said Faith, authoritatively.

'What is it, my wench?' asked Grace. While Lois, feeling as if she had done all the mischief, kept silence.

'Take her away, take her away!' screamed Prudence. 'Look over her shoulder--her left shoulder--the Evil One is there now, I see him stretching over for the half-bitten apple.'

'What is it she says?' said Grace austerely.

'She is dreaming,' said Faith; 'Prudence, hold thy tongue.' And she pinched the child severely, while Lois more tenderly tried to soothe the alarms she felt that she had conjured up.

'Be quiet, Prudence,' said she, 'and go to sleep! I will stay by thee, till thou hast gone off into slumber.'

'No, no! go away!' sobbed Prudence, who was really terrified at first, but was now assuming more alarm than she felt, from the pleasure she received at perceiving herself the centre of attention. 'Faith shall stay by me, not you, wicked English witch!'

So Faith sat by her sister; and Grace, displeased and perplexed, withdrew to her own bed, purposing to inquire more into the matter in the morning. Lois only hoped it might all be forgotten by that time, and resolved never to talk again of such things. But an event happened in the remaining hours of the night to change the current of affairs. While Grace had been absent from her room, her husband had had another paralytic stroke: whether he, too, had been alarmed by that eldritch scream no one could ever know. By the faint light of the rush-candle burning at the bed-side, his wife perceived that a great change had taken place in his aspect on her return: the irregular breathing came almost like snorts--the end was drawing near. The family were roused, and all help given that either the doctor or experience could suggest. But before the late November morning-light, all was ended for Ralph Hickson.

The whole of the ensuing day, they sat or moved in darkened rooms, and spoke few words, and those below their breath. Manasseh kept at home, regretting his father, no doubt, but showing little emotion. Faith was the child that bewailed her loss most grievously; she had a warm heart, hidden away somewhere under her moody exterior, and her father had shown her far more passive kindness than ever her mother had done; for Grace made distinct favorites of Manasseh, her only son, and Prudence, her youngest child. Lois was about as unhappy as any of them; for she had felt strongly drawn towards her uncle as her kindest friend, and the sense of his loss renewed the old sorrow she had experienced at her own parent's death. But she had no time and no place to cry in. On her devolved many of the cares which it would have seemed indecorous in the nearer relatives to interest themselves in enough to take an active part: the change required in their dress, the household preparations for the sad feast of the funeral--Lois had to arrange all under her aunt's stern direction.

But, a day or two afterwards--the last day before the funeral---she went into the yard to fetch in some faggots for the oven; it was a solemn, beautiful, starlit evening, and some sudden sense of desolation in the midst of the vast universe thus revealed touched Lois's heart, and she sat down behind the wood-stack, and cried very plentiful tears.

She was startled by Manasseh, who suddenly turned the corner of the stack, and stood before her.

'Lois crying!'

'Only a little,' she said, rising up, and gathering her bundle of faggots; for she dreaded being questioned by her grim, impassive cousin. To her surprise, he laid his hand on her arm, and said--

'Stop one minute. Why art thou crying, cousin?'

'I don't know,' she said, just like a child questioned in like manner; and she was again on the point of weeping. 'My father was very kind to thee, Lois; I do not wonder that thou grievest after him. But the Lord who taketh away can restore tenfold. I will be as kind as my father-- yea, kinder. This is not a time to talk of marriage and giving in marriage. But after we have buried our dead, I wish to speak to thee.'

Lois did not cry now; but she shrank with affright. What did her cousin mean? She would far rather that he had been angry with her for unreasonable grieving, for folly.

She avoided him carefully--as carefully as she could, without seeming to dread him--for the next few days. Sometimes, she thought it must have been a bad dream; for, if there had been no English lover in the case, no other man in the whole world, she could never have thought of Manasseh as her husband; indeed, till now, there had been nothing in his words or actions to suggest such an idea. Now it had been suggested, there was no telling how much she loathed him. He might be good, and pious--he doubtless was--but his dark, fixed eyes, moving so slowly and heavily, his lank, black hair, his grey, coarse skin, all made her dislike him now--all his personal ugliness and ungainliness struck on her senses with a jar, since those few words spoken behind the hay-stack.

She knew that, sooner or later, the time must come for further discussion of this subject; but, like a coward, she tried to put it off by clinging to her aunt's apron-string, for she was sure that Grace Hickson had far different views for her only son. As, indeed, she had; for she was an ambitious, as well as a religious, woman; and, by an early purchase of land in Salem village, the Hicksons had become wealthy people, without any great exertions of their own--partly, also, by the silent process of accumulation; for they had never cared to change their manner of living, from the time when it had been suitable to a far smaller income than that which they at present enjoyed. So much for worldly circumstances. As for their worldly character, it stood as high. No one could say a word against any of their habits or actions. Their righteousness and godliness were patent to every one's eyes. So Grace Hickson thought herself entitled to pick and choose among the maidens, before she should meet with one fitted to be Manasseh's wife. None in Salem came up to her imaginary standard. She had it in her mind even at this very time, so soon after her husband's death, to go to Boston, and take counsel with the leading ministers there, with worthy Mr Cotton Mather at their head, and see if they could tell her of a well-favored and godly young maiden in their congregations worthy of being the wife of her son. But, besides good looks and godliness, the wench must have good birth and good wealth, or Grace Hickson would have put her contemptuously on one side. When once this paragon was found, and the ministers had approved, Grace anticipated no difficulty on her son's part. So Lois was right in feeling that her aunt would dislike any speech of marriage between Manasseh and herself.

But the girl was brought to bay one day, in this wise. Manasseh had ridden forth on some business, which every one said would occupy him the whole day; but, meeting the man with whom he had to transact his affairs, he returned earlier than any one expected. He missed Lois from the keeping-room, where his sisters were spinning, almost immediately. His mother sat by at her knitting; he could see Nattee in the kitchen through the open door. He was too reserved to ask where Lois was; but he quietly sought till he found her, in the great loft, already piled with winter stores of fruit and vegetables. Her aunt had sent her there to examine the apples one by one, and pick out such as were unsound for immediate use. She was stooping down, and intent upon this work, and was hardly aware of his approach, until she lifted up her head and saw him standing close before her. She dropped the apple she was holding, went a little paler than her wont, and faced him in silence.

'Lois,' he said, 'thou rememberest the words that I spoke while we yet mourned over my father. I think that I am called to marriage now, as the head of this household. And I have seen no maiden so pleasant in my sight as thou art, Lois!' He tried to take her hand. But she put it behind her with a childish shake of her head, and, half crying, said--

'Please, Cousin Manasseh, do not say this to me! I dare say you ought to be married, being the head of the household now; but I don't want to be married. I would rather not.'

'That is well spoken,' replied he; frowning a little, nevertheless. 'I should not like to take to wife an over-forward maiden, ready to jump at wedlock. Besides, the congregation might talk, if we were to be married too soon after my father's death. We have, perchance, said enough, even now. But I wished thee to have thy mind set at case as to thy future well-doing. Thou wilt have leisure to think of it, and to bring thy mind more fully round to it.' Again he held out his hand. This time she took hold of it with a free, frank gesture.

'I owe you somewhat for your kindness to me ever since I came, Cousin Manasseh; and I have no way of paying you but by telling you truly I can love you as a dear friend, if you will let me, but never as a wife.'

He flung her hand away, but did not take his eyes off her face, though his glance was lowering and gloomy. He muttered something which she did not quite hear; and so she went on bravely, although she kept trembling a little, and had much ado to keep from crying.

'Pleae, let me tell you all! There was a young man in Barford---nay, Manasseh, I cannot speak if you are so angry; it is hard work to tell you anyhow--he said that he wanted to marry me; but I was poor, and his father would have none of it; and I do not want to marry any one; but, if I did, it would be'--Her voice dropped, and her blushes told the rest. Manasseh stood looking at her with sullen, hollow eyes, that had a gathering touch of wildness in them; and then he said--

'It is borne in upon me--verily, I see it as in a vision--that thou must be my spouse, and no other man's. Thou canst not escape what is fore-doomed. Months ago, when I set myself to read the old godly books in which my soul used to delight until thy coming; I saw no letter of printer's ink marked upon the page, but I saw a gold and ruddy type of some unknown language, the meaning whereof was whispered into my soul; it was, 'Marry Lois! marry Lois!' And, when my father died, I knew it was the beginning of the end. It is the Lord's will, Lois, and thou canst not escape from it.' And again he would have taken her hand, and drawn her towards him. But this time she eluded him with ready movement.

'I do not acknowledge it to be the Lord's will, Manasseh,' said she. 'It is not "borne in upon me," as you Puritans call it, that I am to be your wife. I am none so set upon wedlock as to take you, even though there be no other chance for me. For I do not care for you as I ought to care for my husband. But I could have cared for you very much as a cousin--as a kind cousin.'

She stopped speaking; she could not choose the right words with which to speak to him of her gratitude and friendliness, which yet could never be any feeling nearer and dearer, no more than two parallel lines can ever meet.

But he was so convinced by what he considered the spirit of prophecy, that Lois was to be his wife, that he felt rather more indignant at what he considered to be her resistance to the preordained decree, than really anxious as to the result. Again he tried to convince her that neither he nor she had any choice in the matter, by saying--

'The voice said unto me "Marry Lois;" and I said, "I will, Lord."'

'But,' Lois replied, 'the voice, as you call it, has never spoken such a word to me.'

'Lois,' he answered solemnly, 'it will speak. And then wilt thou obey, even as Samuel did?'

No; indeed I cannot!' she answered briskly. 'I may take a dream to be the truth, and hear my own fancies, if I think about them too long. But I cannot marry any one from obedience.'

'Lois, Lois, thou art as yet unregenerate; but I have seen thee in a vision as one of the elect, robed in white. As yet thy faith is too weak for thee to obey meekly; but it shall not always be so. I will pray that thou mayest see thy preordained course. Meanwhile, I will smooth away all worldly obstacles.'

'Cousin Manasseh! Cousin Manasseh!' cried Lois after him, as he was leaving the room, 'come back! I cannot put it in strong enough words. Manasseh, there is no power in heaven or earth that can make me love thee enough to marry thee, or to wed thee without such love. And this I say solemnly, because it is better that this should end at once.'

For a moment he was staggered; then he lifted up his hands, and said--

'God forgive thee thy blasphemy! Remember Hazael, who said, "Is thy servant a dog, that he should do this great thing?" and went straight and did it, because his evil courses were fixed and appointed for him from before the foundation of the world. And shall not thy paths be laid out among the godly, as it bath been foretold to me?'

He went away; and for a minute or two Lois felt as if his words must come true, and that, struggle as she would, hate her doom as she would, she must become his wife; and, under the circumstances, many a girl would have succumbed to her apparent fate. Isolated from all previous connections, hearing no word from England, living in the heavy, monotonous routine of a family with one man for head, and this man esteemed a hero by most of those around him, simply because he was the only man in the family--these facts alone would have formed strong presumptions that most girls would have yielded to the offers of such a one. But, besides this, there was much to tell upon the imagination in those days, in that place and time. It was prevalently believed that there were manifestations of spiritual influence--of the direct influence both of good and bad spirits--constantly to be perceived in the course of men's lives. Lots were drawn, as guidance from the Lord; the Bible was opened, and the leaves allowed to fall apart; and the first text the eye fell upon was supposed to be appointed from above as a direction. Sounds were heard that could not be accounted for; they were made by the evil spirits not yet banished from the desert- places of which they had so long held possession. Sights, inexplicable and mysterious, were dimly seen--Satan, in some shape, seeking whom he might devour. And, at the beginning of the long winter season, such whispered tales, such old temptations and hauntings, and devilish terrors, were supposed to be peculiarly rife. Salem was, as it were, snowed up, and left to prey upon itself The long, dark evenings; the dimly-lighted rooms; the creaking passages, where heterogeneous articles were piled away, out of the reach of the keen-piercing frost, and where occasionally, in the dead of night, a sound was heard, as of some heavy falling body, when, next morning, everything appeared to be in its right place (so accustomed are we to measure noises by comparison with themselves, and not with the absolute stillness of the night-season); the white mist, coming nearer and nearer to the windows every evening in strange shapes, like phantoms--all these, and many other circumstances: such as the distant fall of mighty trees in the mysterious forests girdling them round; the faint whoop and cry of some Indian seeking his camp, and unwittingly nearer to the white man's settlement than either he or they would have liked, could they have chosen; the hungry yells of the wild beasts approaching the cattle-pens--these were the things which made that winter life in Salem, in the memorable time of 1691-2, seem strange, and haunted, and terrific to many; peculiarly weird and awful to the English girl, in her first year's sojourn in America.

And now, imagine Lois worked upon perpetually by Manasseh's conviction that it was decreed that she should be his wife, and you will see that she was not without courage and spirit to resist as she did, steadily, firmly, and yet sweetly, Take one instance out of many, when her nerves were subjected to a shock-- slight in relation, it is true; but then remember that she had been all day, and for many days, shut up within doors, in a dull light that at midday was almost dark with a long-continued snowstorm. Evening was coming on, and the wood fire was more cheerful than any of the human beings surrounding it; the monotonous whirr of the smaller spinning-wheels had been going on all day, and the store of flax downstairs was nearly exhausted: when Grace Hickson bade Lois fetch down some more from the store room, before the light so entirely waned away that it could not be found without a candle, and a candle it would be dangerous to carry into that apartment full of combustible materials, especially at this time of hard frost, when every drop of water was locked up and bound in icy hardness. So Lois went, half-shrinking from the long passage that led to the stairs leading up into the store room, for it was in this passage that the strange night-sounds were heard, which every one had begun to notice, and speak about in lowered tones. She sang, however, as she went, 'to keep her courage up,' in a subdued voice, the evening hymn she had so often sung in Barford church--

'Glory to Thee, my God, this night;' and so it was, I suppose, that she never heard the breathing or motion of any creature near her, till, just as she was loading herself with flax to carry down, she heard some one--it was Manasseh--say close to her ear; 'Has the voice spoken yet? Speak, Lois! Has the voice spoken yet to thee--that speaketh to me day and night, "Marry Lois"?'

She started and turned a little sick, but spoke almost directly in a brave, clear manner--

'No, Cousin Manasseh! And it never will.'

'Then I must wait yet longer,' he replied hoarsely, as if to himself. 'But all submission--all submission.'

At last, a break came upon the monotony of the long, dark winter. The parishioners once more raised the discussion whether--the parish extending as it did--it was not absolutely necessary for Pastor Tappau to have help. This question had been mooted once before; and then Pastor Tappau had acquiesced in the necessity, and all had gone on smoothly for some months after the appointment of his assistant; until a feeling had sprung up on the part of the elder minister, which might have been called jealousy of the younger, if so godly a man as Pastor Tappau could have been supposed to entertain so evil a passion. However that might be, two parties were speedily formed; the younger and more ardent being in favor of Mr Nolan, the elder and more persistent---and, at the time, the more numerous--clinging to the old, grey-headed, dogmatic Mr Tappau, who had married them, baptized their children, and was to them, literally, as a 'pillar of the church.' So Mr Nolan left Salem, carrying away with him, possibly, more hearts than that of Faith Hickson's; but certainly she had never been the same creature since.

But now--Christmas, 1691--one or two of the older members of the congregation being dead, and some who were younger men having come to settle in Salem--Mr Tappau being also older, and, some charitably supposed, wiser--a fresh effort had been made, and Mr Nolan was returning to labour in ground apparently smoothed over. Lois had taken a keen interest in all the proceedings for Faith's sake--far more than the latter did for herself, any spectator would have said. Faith's wheel never went faster or slower, her thread never broke, her color never came, her eyes were never uplifted with sudden interest, all the time these discussions respecting Mr Nolan's return were going on. But Lois, after the hint given by Prudence, had found a clue to many a sigh and look of despairing sorrow, even without the help of Nattee's improvised songs, in which, under strange allegories, the helpless love of her favorite was told to ears heedless of all meaning, except those of the tenderhearted and sympathetic Lois. Occasionally, she heard a strange chant of the old Indian woman's--half in her own language, half in broken English--droned over some simmering pipkin, from which the smell was, to say the least, unearthly. Once, on perceiving this odor in the keeping-room, Grace Hickson suddenly exclaimed--

Nattee is at her heathen ways again; we shall have some mischief unless she is stayed.'

But Faith, moving quicker than ordinary, said something about putting a stop to it, and so forestalled her mother's evident intention of going into the kitchen. Faith shut the door between the two rooms, and entered upon some remonstrance with Nattee; but no one could hear the words used. Faith and Nattee seemed more bound together by love and common interest than any other two among the self-contained individuals comprising this household. Lois sometimes felt as if her presence, as a third, interrupted some confidential talk between her cousin and the old servant. And yet she was fond of Faith, and could almost think that Faith liked her more than she did either mother, brother, or sister; for the first two were indifferent as to any unspoken feelings, while Prudence delighted in discovering them, only to make an amusement to herself out of them.

One day, Lois was sitting by herself at her sewing-table, while Faith and Nattee were holding one of their secret conclaves, from which Lois felt herself to be tacitly excluded: when the outer door opened, and a tall, pale young man, in the strict professional habit of a minister, entered. Lois sprang up with a smile and a look of welcome for Faith's sake; for this must be the Mr Nolan whose name had been on the tongue of every one for days, and who was, as Lois knew, expected to arrive the day before.

He seemed half-surprised at the glad alacrity with which he was received by this stranger: possibly, he had not heard of the English girl who was an inmate in the house where formerly he had seen only grave, solemn, rigid, or heavy faces, and had been received with a stiff form of welcome, very different from the blushing, smiling, dimpled looks that innocently met him with the greeting almost of an old acquaintance. Lois, having placed a chair for him, hastened out to call Faith, never doubting but that the feeling which her cousin entertained for the young pastor was mutual, although it might be unrecognized in its full depth by either.

'Faith!' said she, bright and breathless. 'Guess--No,' checking herself to an assumed unconsciousness of any particular importance likely to be affixed to her words; 'Mr Nolan, the new pastor, is in the keeping-room. He has asked for my aunt and Manasseh. My aunt is gone to the prayer-meeting at Pastor Tappau's, and Manasseh is away.' Lois went on speaking, to give Faith time; for the girl had become deadly white at the intelligence, while, at the same time, her eyes met the keen, cunning eyes of the old Indian with a peculiar look of half-wondering awe; while Nattee's looks expressed triumphant satisfaction.

'Go,' said Lois, smoothing Faith's hair, and kissing the white, cold cheek, 'or he will wonder why no one comes to see him, and perhaps think he is not welcome.' Faith went without another word into the keeping-room, and shut the door of communication. Nattee and Lois were left together. Lois felt as happy as if some piece of good fortune had befallen herself. For the time, her growing dread of Manasseh's wild, ominous persistence in his suit, her aunt's coldness, her own loneliness, were all forgotten, and she could almost have danced with joy. Nattee laughed aloud, and talked and chuckled to herself.'Old Indian woman great mystery. Old Indian woman sent hither and thither; go where she is told, where she hears with her ears. But old Indian woman'--and here she drew herself up, and the expression of her face quite changed--'know how to call, and then white man must come; and old Indian woman have spoken never a word, and white man have heard nothing with his ears.' So the old crone muttered.

All this time, things were going on very differently in the keeping- room to what Lois imagined. Faith sat stiller even than usual; her eyes downcast, her words few. A quick observer might have noticed a certain tremulousness about her hands, and an occasional twitching throughout all her frame. But Pastor Nolan was not a keen observer upon this occasion; he was absorbed with his own little wonders and perplexities. His wonder was that of a carnal man--who that pretty stranger might be, who had seemed, on his first coming, so glad to see him, but had vanished instantly, apparently not to reappear. And, indeed, I am not sure if his perplexity was not that of a carnal man rather than that of a godly minister, for this was his dilemma. It was the custom of Salem (as we have already seen) for the minister, on entering a household for the visit which, among other people and in other times, would have been termed a 'morning call,' to put up a prayer for the eternal welfare of the family under whose roof-tree he was. Now this prayer was expected to be adapted to the individual character, joys, sorrows, wants, and failings of every member present; and here was he, a young pastor, alone with a young woman; and he thought--vain thoughts, perhaps, but still very natural--that the implied guesses at her character, involved in the minute supplications above described, would be very awkward in a tete-a-tete prayer; so, whether it was his wonder or his perplexity, I do not know, but he did not contribute much to the conversation for some time, and at last, by a sudden burst of courage and impromptu hit, he cut the Gordian knot by making the usual proposal for prayer and adding to it a request that the household might be summoned. In came Lois, quiet and decorous; in came Nattee, all one impassive, stiff piece of wood--no look of intelligence or trace of giggling near her countenance. Solemnly recalling each wandering thought, Pastor Nolan knelt in the midst of these three to pray. He was a good and truly religious man, whose name here is the only thing disguised, and played his part bravely in the awful trial to which he was afterwards subjected; and if, at the time, before he went through his fiery persecutions, the human fancies which beset all young hearts came across his, we at this day know that these fancies are no sin. But now he prays in earnest, prays so heartily for himself, with such a sense of his own spiritual need and spiritual failings, that each one of his hearers feels as if a prayer and a supplication had gone up for each of them. Even Nattee muttered the few words she knew of the Lord's Prayer; gibberish though the disjointed nouns and verbs might be, the poor creature said them because she was stirred to unwonted reverence. As for Lois, she rose up comforted and strengthened, as no special prayers of Pastor Tappau had ever made her feel. But Faith was sobbing, sobbing aloud, almost hysterically, and made no effort to rise, but lay on her outstretched arms spread out upon the settle. Lois and Pastor Nolan looked at each other for an instant. Then Lois said--

'Sir, you must go. My cousin has not been strong for some time, and doubtless she needs more quiet than she has had today.'

Pastor Nolan bowed, and left the house; but in a moment he returned. Half-opening the door, but without entering, he said--

'I come back to ask, if perchance I may call this evening to inquire how young Mistress Hickson finds herself?'

But Faith did not hear this; she was sobbing louder than ever.

'Why did you send him away, Lois? I should have been better directly, and it is so long since I have seen him.'

She had her face hidden as she uttered these words and Lois could not hear them distinctly. She bent her head down by her cousin's on the settle, meaning to ask her to repeat what she had said. But in the irritation of the moment, and prompted possibly by some incipient jealousy, Faith pushed Lois away so violently that the latter was hurt against the hard, sharp corner of the wooden settle. Tears came into her eyes; not so much because her cheek was bruised, as because of the surprised pain she felt at this repulse from the cousin towards whom she was feeling so warmly and kindly, just for the moment, Lois was as angry as any child could have been; but some of the words of Pastor Nolan's prayer yet rang in her ears, and she thought it would be a shame if she did not let them sink into her heart. She dared not, however, stoop again to caress Faith, but stood quietly by her, sorrowfully waiting; until a step at the outer door caused Faith to rise quickly, and rush into the kitchen, leaving Lois to bear the brunt of the new-comer. It was Manasseh, returned from hunting. He had been two days away, in company with other young men belonging to Salem. It was almost the only occupation which could draw him out of his secluded habits. He stopped suddenly at the door on seeing Lois, and alone; for she had avoided him of late in every possible way.

'Where is my mother?'

'At a prayer-meeting at Pastor Tappau's. She has taken Prudence. Faith has left the room this minute. I will call her.' And Lois was going towards the kitchen, when he placed himself between her and the door.

'Lois,' said he, 'the rime is going by, and I cannot wait much longer. The visions come thick upon me, and my sight grows clearer and clearer. Only this last night, camping out in the woods, I saw in my soul, between sleeping and waking, the spirit come and offer thee two lots; and the color of the one was white, like a bride's, and the other was black and red, which is, being interpreted, a violent death. And, when thou didst choose the latter, the spirit said unto me, "Come!" and I came, and did as I was bidden. I put it on thee with mine own hands, as it is preordained, if thou wilt not hearken unto the voice and be my wife. And when the black and red dress fell to the ground, thou wert even as a corpse three days old. Now, be advised, Lois, in time! Lois, my cousin, I have seen it in a vision, and my soul cleaveth unto thee--I would fain spare thee.'

He was really in earnest--in passionate earnest; whatever his visions, as he called them, might be, he believed in them, and this belief gave something of unselfishness to his love for Lois. This she felt at this moment, if she had never done so before; and it seemed like a contrast to the repulse she had just met with from his sister. He had drawn near her, and now he took hold of her hand, repeating in his wild, pathetic, dreamy way--

'And the voice said unto me, "Marry Lois!"' And Lois was more inclined to soothe and reason with him than she had ever been before, since the first time of his speaking to her on the subject--when Grace Hickson and Prudence entered the room from the passage. They had returned from the prayer-meeting by the back way, which had prevented the sound of their approach from being heard.

But Manasseh did not stir or look round; he kept his eyes fixed on Lois, as if to note the effect of his words. Grace came hastily forwards and, lifting up her strong right arm, smote their joined hands in twain, in spite of the fervour of Manasseh's grasp.

'What means this?' said she, addressing herself more to Lois than to her son, anger flashing out of her deep-set eyes.

Lois waited for Manasseh to speak. He seemed, but a few minutes before, to be more gentle and less threatening than he had been of late on this subject, and she did not wish to irritate him. But he did not speak, and her aunt stood angrily waiting for an answer.

'At any rate,' thought Lois, 'it will put an end to the thought in his mind, when my aunt speaks out about it.'

'My cousin seeks me in marriage,' said Lois.

'Thee!' and Grace struck out in the direction of her niece with a gesture of supreme contempt. But now Manasseh spoke forth--

'Yea! it is preordained. The voice has said it, and the spirit has brought her to me as my bride.'

'Spirit! an evil spirit then! A good spirit would have chosen out for thee a godly maiden of thine own people, and not a prelatist and a stranger like this girl. A pretty return, Mistress Lois, for all our kindness!'

'Indeed, Aunt Hickson, I have done all I could--Cousin Manasseh knows it--to show him I can be none of his. I have told him,' said she, blushing, but determined to say the whole out at once, 'that I am all but troth-plight to a young man of our own village at home; and even putting all that on one side, I wish not for marriage at present.'

'Wish rather for conversion and regeneration! Marriage is an unseemly word in the mouth of a maiden. As for Manasseh, I will take reason with him in private; and, meanwhile, if thou hast spoken truly, throw not thyself in his path, as I have noticed thou hast done but too often of late.'

Lois's heart burnt within her at this unjust accusation, for she knew how much she had dreaded and avoided her cousin, and she almost looked to him to give evidence that her aunt's last words were not true. But, instead, he recurred to his one fixed idea, and said--

'Mother, listen! If I wed not Lois, both she and I die within the year. I care not for life; before this, as you know, I have sought for death' (Grace shuddered, and was for a moment subdued by some recollection of past horror); 'but, if Lois were my wife, I should live, and she would be spared from what is the other lot. That whole vision grows clearer to me, day by day. Yet, when I try to know whether I am one of the elect, all is dark. The mystery of Free-Will and Fore-Knowledge is a mystery of Satan's devising, not of God's.'

'Alas, my son! Satan is abroad among the brethren even now; but let the old vexed topics rest! Sooner than fret thyself again, thou shalt have Lois to be thy wife, though my heart was set far differently for thee.'

'No, Manasseh,' said Lois. 'I love you well as a cousin, but wife of yours I can never be. Aunt Hickson, it is not well to delude him so. I say, if ever I marry man, I am troth-plight to one in England.'

'Tush, child! I am your guardian in my dead husband's place. Thou thinkest thyself so great a prize that I could clutch at thee whether or no, I doubt not. I value thee not, save as a medicine for Manasseh, if his mind get disturbed again, as I have noted signs of late.'

This, then, was the secret explanation of much that had alarmed her in her cousin's manner: and, if Lois had been a physician of modern times, she might have traced somewhat of the same temperament in his sisters as well--in Prudence's lack of natural feeling and impish delight in mischief, in Faith's vehemence of unrequited love. But, as yet, Lois did not know, any more than

Faith, that the attachment of the latter to Mr Nolan was not merely unreturned, but even unperceived, by the young minister.

He came, it is true--came often to the house, sat long with the family, and watched them narrowly, but took no especial notice of Faith. Lois perceived this, and grieved over it; Nattee perceived it, and was indignant at it, long before Faith slowly acknowledged it to herself, and went to Nattee the Indian woman, rather than to Lois her cousin, for sympathy and counsel.

'He cares not for me,' said Faith. 'He cares more for Lois's little finger than for my whole body,' the girl moaned out, in the bitter pain of jealousy.

'Hush thee, hush thee, prairie-bird! How can he build a nest, when the old bird has got all the moss and the feathers?' Wait till the Indian has found means to send the old bird flying far away.' This was the mysterious comfort Nattee gave.

Grace Hickson took some kind of charge over Manasseh that relieved Lois of much of her distress at his strange behaviour. Yet, at times, he escaped from his mother's watchfulness, and in such opportunities he would always seek Lois, entreating her, as of old, to marry him--- sometimes pleading his love for her, oftener speaking wildly of his visions and the voices which he heard foretelling a terrible futurity.

We have now to do with events which were taking place in Salem, beyond the narrow circle of the Hickson family; but, as they only concern us in as far as they bore down in their consequences on the future of those who formed part of it, I shall go over the narrative very briefly. The town of Salem had lost by death, within a very short time preceding the commencement of my story, nearly all its venerable men and leading citizens--men of ripe wisdom and sound counsel. The people had hardly yet recovered from the shock of their loss, as one by one the patriarchs of the primitive little community had rapidly followed each other to the grave. They had been loved as fathers, and looked up to as judges in the land. The first bad effect of their loss was seen in the heated dissention which sprang up between Pastor Tappau and the candidate Nolan. It had been apparently healed over; but Mr Nolan had not been many weeks in Salem, after his second coming, before the strife broke out afresh, and alienated many for life who had till then been bound together by the ties of friendship or relationship. Even in the Hickson family something of this feeling soon sprang up; Grace being a vehement partisan of the elder pastor's more gloomy doctrines, while Faith was a passionate, if a powerless, advocate of Mr Nolan. Manasseh's growing absorption in his own fancies, and imagined gift of prophecy, making him comparatively indifferent to all outward events, did not tend to either the fulfillment of his visions, or the elucidation of the dark mysterious doctrines over which he had pondered too long for the health either of his mind or body; while Prudence delighted in irritating every one by her advocacy of the views of thinking to which they were most opposed, and relating every gossiping story to the person most likely to disbelieve, and to be indignant at, what she told with an assumed unconsciousness of any such effect to be produced. There was much talk of the congregational difficulties and dissensions being carried up to the general court; and each party naturally hoped that, if such were the course of events, the opposing pastor and that portion of the congregation which adhered to him might be worsted in the struggle.

Such was the state of things in the township, when, one day towards the end of the month of February, Grace Hickson returned from the weekly prayer-meeting, which it was her custom to attend at Pastor Tappau's house, in a state of extreme excitement. On her entrance into her own house she sat down, rocking her body backwards and forwards, and praying to herself. Both Faith and Lois stopped their spinning, in wonder at her agitation, before either of them ventured to address her. At length Faith rose, and spoke--

'Mother, what is it? Hath anything happened of any evil nature?'

The brave, stern old woman's face was blenched, and her eyes were almost set in horror, as she prayed; the great drops running down her cheeks.

It seemed almost as if she had to make a struggle to recover her sense of the present homely accustomed fife, before she could find words to answer--

Evil nature! Daughters, Satan is abroad--is close to us; I have this very hour seen him afflict two innocent children, as of old he troubled those who were possessed by him in Judea. Hester and Abigail Tappau have been contorted and convulsed by him and his servants into such shapes as I am afeared to think on; and when their father, godly Mr Tappau, began to exhort and to pray, their howlings were like the wild beasts of the field. Satan is of a truth let loose among us. The girls kept calling upon him, as if he were even then present among us. Abigail screeched out that he stood at my very back in the guise of a black man; and truly, as I turned round at her words, I saw a creature like a shadow vanishing, and turned all of a cold sweat. Who knows where he is now? Faith, lay straws across the door-sill!'

'But, if he be already entered in,' asked Prudence,' may not that make it difficult for him to depart?'

Her mother, taking no notice of her question, went on rocking herself, and praying, till again she broke out into narration--

'Reverend Mr Tappau says, that only last night he heard a sound as of a heavy body dragged all through his house by some strong power; once it was thrown against his bedroom door, and would, doubtless, have broken it in, if he had not prayed fervently and aloud at that very time; and a shriek went up at his prayer that made his hair stand on end; and this morning all the crockery in the house was found broken and piled up in the middle of the kitchen floor, and Pastor Tappau says that, as soon as he began to ask a blessing on the morning's meal, Abigail and Hester cried out, as if some one was pinching them. Lord, have mercy upon us all! Satan is of a truth let loose.'

'They sound like the old stories I used to hear in Barford,' said Lois, breathless with affright.

Faith seemed less alarmed; but then her dislike to Pastor Tappau was so great, that she could hardly sympathise with any misfortunes that befell him or his family.

Towards evening Mr Nolan came in. In general, so high did party spirit run, Grace Hickson only tolerated his visits, finding herself often engaged at such hours, and being too much abstracted in thought to show him the ready hospitality which was one of her most prominent virtues. But today, both as bringing the latest intelligence of the new horrors sprung up in Salem, and as being one of the Church militant (or what the Puritans considered as equivalent to the Church militant) against Satan, he was welcomed by her in an unusual manner.

He seemed oppressed with the occurrences of the day; at first it appeared to be almost a relief to him to sit still, and cogitate upon them, and his hosts were becoming almost impatient for him to say something more than mere monosyllables, when he began--

'Such a day as this I pray that I may never see again. It is as if the devils, whom our Lord banished into the herd of swine, had been permitted to come again upon the earth. And I would it were only the lost spirits who were tormenting us; but I much fear that certain of those whom we have esteemed as God's people have sold their souls to Satan, for the sake of a little of his evil power, whereby they may afflict others for a time. Elder Sherringham bath lost this very day a good and valuable horse, wherewith he used to drive his family to meeting.'

'Perchance,' said Lois, 'the horse died of some natural disease.'

'True,' said Pastor Nolan; 'but I was going on to say, that, as he entered into his house, full of dolour at the loss of his beast, a mouse ran in before him so sudden that it almost tripped him up, though an instant before there was no such thing to be seen; and he caught it with his shoe and hit it, and it cried out like a human creature in pain, and straight ran up the chimney, caring nothing for the hot flame and smoke.'

Manasseh listened greedily to all this story; and, when it was ended he smote his breast, and prayed aloud for deliverance from the power of the Evil One; and he continually went on praying at intervals through the evening, with every mark of abject terror on his face and in his manner--he, the bravest, most daring hunter in all the settlement. Indeed, all the family huddled together in silent fear, scarcely finding any interest in the usual household occupations. Faith and Lois sat with arms entwined, as in days before the former had become jealous of the latter; Prudence asked low, fearful questions of her mother and of the pastor as to the creatures that were abroad, and the ways in which they afflicted others; and, when Grace besought the minister to pray for her and her household, he made a long and passionate supplication that none of that little flock might ever so far fall away into hopeless perdition as to be guilty of the sin without forgiveness--the Sin of Witchcraft.

Chapter 3

'The Sin of Witchcraft.' We read about it, we look on it from the outside; but we can hardly realize the terror it induced. Every impulsive or unaccustomed action, every little nervous affection, every ache or pain was noticed, not merely by those around the sufferer, but by the person himself, whoever he might be, that was acting, or being acted upon, in any but the most simple and ordinary manner. He or she (for it was most frequently a woman or girl that was the supposed subject) felt a desire for some unusual kind of food-- some unusual motion or rest--her hand twitched, her foot was asleep, or her leg had the cramp; and the dreadful question immediately suggested itself, 'Is any one possessing an evil power over me; by the help of Satan?' and perhaps they went on to think, 'It is bad enough to feel that my holy can he made to suffer through the power of some unknown evil-wisher to me; but what if Satan gives them still further power, and they can touch my soul, and inspire me with loathful thoughts leading me into crimes which at present I abhor?' and so on, till the very dread of what might happen, and the constant dwelling of the thoughts, even with horror, upon certain possibilities, or what were esteemed such, really brought about the corruption of imagination at last, which at first they had shuddered at. Moreover, there was a sort of uncertainty as to who might be infected--not unlike the overpowering dread of the plague, which made some shrink from their best-beloved with irrepressible fear. The brother or sister, who was the dearest friend of their childhood and youth, might now be bound in some mysterious deadly pack with evil spirits of the most horrible kind--who could tell? And in such a case it became a duty, a sacred duty, to give up the earthly body which bad been once so loved, but which was now the habitation of a soul corrupt and horrible in its evil inclinations. Possibly, terror of death might bring on confession, and repentance, and purification. Or if it did not, why, away with the evil creature, the witch, out of the world, down to the kingdom of the master, whose bidding was done on earth in all manner of corruption and torture of God's creatures! There were others who, to these more simple, if more ignorant, feelings of horror at witches and witchcraft, added the desire, conscious or unconscious, of revenge on those whose conduct had been in any way displeasing to them. Where evidence takes a supernatural character, there is no disproving it. This argument comes up: 'You have only the natural powers; I have supernatural. You admit the existence of the supernatural by the condemnation of this very crime of witchcraft. You hardly know the limits of the natural powers; how, then, can you define the supernatural? I say that in the dead of night, when my body seemed to all present to be lying in quiet sleep, I was, in the most complete and wakeful consciousness, present in my body at an assembly of witches and wizards, with Satan at their head; that I was by them tortured in my body, because my soul would not acknowledge him as its king; and that I witnessed such and such deeds. What the nature of the appearance was that took the semblance of myself, sleeping quietly in my bed, I know not; but, admitting, as you do, the possibility of witchcraft, you cannot disprove my evidence.' The evidence might be given truly or falsely, as the person witnessing believed it or not; but every one must see what immense and terrible power was abroad for revenge. Then, again, the accused themselves ministered to the horrible panic abroad. Some, in dread of death, confessed from cowardice to the imaginary crimes of which they were accused, and of which they were promised a pardon on confession. Some, weak and terrified, came honestly to believe in their own guilt, through the diseases of imagination which were sure to be engendered at such a time as this.

Lois sat spinning with Faith. Both were silent, pondering over the stories that were abroad. Lois spoke first.

'Oh, Faith! this country is worse than ever England was, even in the days of Master Matthew Hopkinson, the witch-finder. I grow frightened of every one, I think. I even get afeared sometimes of Nattee!'

Faith colored a little. Then she asked--

'Why? What should make you distrust the Indian woman?'

'Oh! I am ashamed of my fear as soon as it arises in my mind. But, you know, her look and color were strange to me when I first came; and she is not a christened woman; and they tell stories of Indian wizards; and I know not what the mixtures are which she is sometimes stirring over the fire, nor the meaning of the strange chants she sings to herself. And once I met her in the dusk, just close by Pastor Tappau's house, in company with Hota, his servant--it was just before we heard of the sore disturbance in his house--and I have wondered if she had aught to do with it.'

Faith sat very still, as if thinking. At last she said--

'If Nattee has powers beyond what you and I have, she will not use them for evil; at least not evil to those whom she loves.'

'That comforts me but little,' said Lois. 'If she has powers beyond what she ought to have, I dread her, though I have done her no evil; nay, though I could almost say she bore me a kindly feeling. But such powers are only given by the Evil One; and the proof thereof is, that, as you imply, Nattee would use them on those who offend her.'

'And why should she not?' asked Faith, lifting her eyes, and flashing heavy fire out of them, at the question.

'Because,' said Lois, not seeing Faith's glance, 'we are told to pray for them that despitefully use us, and to do good to them that persecute us. But poor Nattee is not a christened woman. I would that Mr Nolan would baptize her: it would, maybe, take her out of the power of Satan's temptations.'

'Are you never tempted?' asked Faith half-scornfully; 'and yet I doubt not you were well baptized!'

'True,' said Lois sadly; 'I often do very wrong; but, perhaps, I might have done worse, if the holy form had not been observed.'

They were again silent for a time.

'Lois,' said Faith, 'I did not mean any offence'. But do you never feel as if you would give up all that future life, of which the parsons talk, and which seems so vague and so distant, for a few years of real, vivid blessedness, to begin tomorrow--this hour--this minute? Oh! I could think of happiness for which I would willingly give up all those misty chances of heaven'--

'Faith, Faith!' cried Lois in terror, holding her hand before her cousin's mouth, and looking around in fright. 'Hush! you know not who may be listening; you are putting yourself in his power.'

But Faith pushed her hand away, and said, 'Lois, I believe in him no more than I believe in heaven. Both may exist; but they are so far away that I defy them. Why all this ado about Mr Tappau's house--- promise me never to tell living creature, and I will tell you a secret.'

'No!' said Lois, terrified. 'I dread all secrets. I will hear none. I will do all that I can for you, Cousin Faith, in any way; but just at this time, I strive to keep my life and thoughts within the strictest bounds of godly simplicity, and I dread pledging myself to aught that is hidden and secret.

'As you will, cowardly girl, full of terrors, which, if you had listened to me, might have been lessened, if not entirely done away with.' And Faith would not utter another word, though Lois tried meekly to entice her into conversation on some other subject.

The rumour of witchcraft was like the echo of thunder among the hills. It had broken out in Mr Tappau's house, and his two little daughters were the first supposed to be bewitched; but round about, from every quarter of the town, came in accounts of sufferers by witchcraft. There was hardly a family without one of these supposed victims. Then arose a growl and menaces of vengeance from many a household--menaces deepened, not daunted, by the terror and mystery of the suffering that gave rise to them.

At length a day was appointed when, after solemn fasting and prayer, Mr Tappau invited the neighboring ministers and all godly people to assemble at his house, and unite with him in devoting a day to solemn religious services, and to supplication for the deliverance of his children, and those similarly afflicted, from the power of the Evil One. All Salem poured out towards the house of the minister. There was a look of excitement on all their faces; eagerness and horror were depicted on many, while stern resolution, amounting to determined cruelty, if the occasion arose, was seen on others.

In the midst of the prayer, Hester Tappau, the younger girl, fell into convulsions; fit after fit came on, and her screams mingled with the shrieks and cries of the assembled congregation. In the first pause, when the child was partially recovered, when the people stood around, exhausted and breathless, her father, the Pastor Tappau, lifted his right hand, and adjured her, in the name of the Trinity, to say who tormented her. There was a dead silence; not a creature stirred of all those hundreds. Hester turned wearily and uneasily, and moaned out the name of Hota, her father's Indian servant. Hota was present, apparently as much interested as any one; indeed, she had been busying herself much in bringing remedies to the suffering child. But now she stood aghast, transfixed, while her name was caught up and shouted out in tones of reprobation and hatred by all the crowd around her. Another moment, and they would have fallen upon the trembling creature and torn her limb from limb--pale, dusky, shivering Hota, half guilty- looking from her very bewilderment. But Pastor Tappau, that gaunt, grey man, lifting himself to his utmost height, signed to them to go back, to keep still while he addressed them; and then he told them that instant vengeance was not just, deliberate punishment; that there would be need of conviction, perchance of confession; he hoped for some redress for his suffering children from her revelations, if she were brought to confession. They must leave the culprit in his hands, and in those of his brother ministers, that they might wrestle with Satan before delivering her up to the civil power. He spoke well; for he spoke from the heart of a father seeing his children exposed to dreadful and mysterious suffering, and firmly believing that he now held the clue in his hand which should ultimately release them and their fellow-sufferers. And the congregation moaned themselves into unsatisfied submission, and listened to his long, passionate prayer, which he uplifted even while the hapless Hota stood there, guarded and bound by two men, who glared at her like blood-hounds ready to slip, even while the prayer ended in the words of the merciful Savior.

Lois sickened and shuddered at the whole scene; and this was no intellectual shuddering at the folly and superstition of the people, but tender moral shuddering at the sight of guilt which she believed in, and at the evidence of men's hatred and abhorrence, which, when shown even to the guilty, troubled and distressed her merciful heart. She followed her aunt and cousins out into the open air, with downcast eyes and pale face. Grace Hickson was going home with a feeling of triumphant relief at the detection of the guilty one. Faith alone seemed uneasy and disturbed beyond her wont; for Manasseh received the whole transaction as the fulfillment of a prophecy, and Prudence was excited by the novel scene into a state of discordant high spirits.

'I am quite as old as Hester Tappau,' she said; 'her birthday is in September and mine in October.'

'What has that to do with it?' said Faith sharply.

'Nothing; only she seemed such a little thing for all those grave ministers to be praying for, and so many folk come from a distance; some from Boston, they said, all for her sake, as it were. Why, didst thou see, it was godly Mr Henwick that held her head when she wriggled so, and old Madam Holbrook had herself helped up on a chair to see the better? I wonder how long I might wriggle, before great and godly folk would take so much notice of me? But, I suppose, that comes of being a pastor's daughter. She'll be so set up, there'll be no speaking to her now. Faith! thinkest thou that Hota really had bewitched her? She gave me corn-cakes the last time I was at Pastor Tappau's, just like any other woman, only, perchance, a trifle more good-natured; and to think of her being a witch after all!'

But Faith seemed in a hurry to reach home, and paid no attention to Prudence's talking. Lois hastened on with Faith; for Manasseh was walking alongside of his mother, and she kept steady to her plan of avoiding him, even though she pressed her company upon Faith, who had seemed of late desirous of avoiding her.

That evening the news spread through Salem, that Hota had confessed her sin--had acknowledged that she was a witch. Nattee was the first to hear the intelligence. She broke into the room where the girls were sitting with Grace Hickson, solemnly doing nothing, because of the great prayer-meeting in the morning, and cried out, 'Mercy, mercy, mistress, everybody! take care of poor Indian Nattee, who never do wrong, but for mistress and the family! Hota one bad, wicked witch; she say so herself; oh, me! oh, me!' and, stooping over Faith, she said something in a low, miserable tone of voice, of which Lois only heard the word 'torture.' But Faith heard all, and, turning very pale, half-accompanied, half-led Nattee back to her kitchen.

Presently, Grace Hickson came in. She had been out to see a neighbor: it will not do to say that so godly a woman had been gossiping; and, indeed, the subject of the conversation she had held was of too serious and momentous a nature for me to employ a light word to designate it. There was all the listening to, and repeating of, small details and rumors, in which the speakers have no concern, that constitutes gossiping; but, in this instance, all trivial facts and speeches might be considered to bear such dreadful significance, and might have so ghastly an ending, that such whispers were occasionally raised to a tragic importance. Every fragment of intelligence that related to Mr Tappau's household was eagerly snatched at: how his dog howled all one long night through, and could not be stilled; how his cow suddenly failed in her milk, only two months after she had calved; how his memory had forsaken him one morning for a minute or two, in repeating the Lord's Prayer, and he had even omitted a clause thereof in his sudden perturbation; and how all these forerunners of his children's strange illness might now be interpreted and understood--- this had formed the staple of the conversation between Grace Hickson and her friends. There had arisen a dispute among them at last, as to how far these subsections to the power of the Evil One were to be considered as a judgment upon Pastor Tappau for some sin on his part; and if so, what? It was not an unpleasant discussion, although there was considerable difference of opinion; for, as none of the speakers had had their families so troubled, it was rather a proof that they had none of them committed any sin. In the midst of this talk, one, entering in from the street, brought the news that Hota had confessed all--had owned to signing a certain little red book which Satan had presented to her--had been present at impious sacraments--had ridden through the air to Newbury Falls--and, in fact, had assented to all the questions which the elders and magistrates, carefully reading over the confessions of the witches who had formerly been tried in England, in order that they might not omit a single inquiry, had asked of her. More she had owned to, but things of inferior importance, and partaking more of the nature of earthly tricks than of spiritual power. She had spoken of carefully-adjusted strings, by which all the crockery in Pastor Tappau's house could be pulled down or disturbed; but of such intelligible malpractices the gossips of Salem took little heed. One of them said that such an action showed Satan's prompting; but they all preferred to listen to the grander guilt of the blasphemous sacraments and supernatural rides. The narrator ended with saying that Hota was to be hung the next morning, in spite of her confession, even although her life had been promised to her if she acknowledged her sin; for it was well to make an example of the first-discovered witch, and it was also well that she was an Indian, a heathen, whose life would be no great loss to the community. Grace Hickson on this spoke out. It was well that witches should perish off the face of the earth, Indian or English, heathen or, worse, a baptized Christian who had betrayed the Lord, even as Judas did, and had gone over to Satan. For her part, she wished that the first-discovered witch had been a member of a godly English household, that it might be seen of all men that religious folk were willing to cut off the right hand, and pluck out the right eye, if tainted with the devilish sin. She spoke sternly and well. The last corner said that her words might be brought to proof, for it had been whispered that Hota had named others, and some from the most religious families of Salem, whom she had seen among the unholy communicants at the sacraments of the Evil One. And Grace replied that she would answer for it, all godly folk would stand the proof, and quench all natural affection rather than that such a sin should grow and spread among them. She herself had a weak bodily dread of witnessing the violent death even of an animal; but she would not let that deter her from standing amidst those who cast the accursed creature out from among them on the morrow morning.

Contrary to her wont, Grace Hickson told her family much of this conversation. It was a sign of her excitement on the subject that she thus spoke, and the excitement spread in different forms through her family. Faith was flushed and restless, wandering between the keeping- room and the kitchen, and questioning her mother particularly as to the more extraordinary parts of Hota's confession, as if she wished to satisfy herself that the Indian witch had really done those horrible and mysterious deeds.

Lois shivered and trembled with affright at the narration, and at the idea that such things were possible. Occasionally she found herself wandering off into sympathetic thought for the woman who was to die, abhorred of all men, and unpardoned by God, to whom she had been so fearful a traitor, and who was now, at this very time--when Lois sat among her kindred by the warm and cheerful firelight, anticipating many peaceful, perchance happy, morrows-- solitary, shivering, panic- stricken, guilty, with none to stand by her and exhort her, shut up in darkness between the cold walls of the town prison. But Lois almost shrank from sympathizing with so loathsome an accomplice of Satan, and prayed for forgiveness for her charitable thought; and yet, again, she remembered the tender spirit of the Savior, and allowed herself to fall into pity, till at last her sense of right and wrong became so bewildered that she could only leave all to God's disposal, and just ask that he would take all creatures and all events into His hands.

Prudence was as bright as if she were listening to some merry story-- curious as to more than her mother would tell her--seeming to have no particular terror of witches or witchcraft, and yet to be especially desirous to accompany her mother the next morning to the hanging. Lois shrank from the cruel, eager face of the young girl, as she begged her mother to allow her to go. Even Grace was disturbed and perplexed by her daughter's pertinacity.

'No,' she said. 'Ask me no more! Thou shalt not go. Such sights are not for the young. I go, and I sicken at the thoughts of it. But I go to show that I, a Christian woman, take God's part against the devil's. Thou shalt not go, I tell thee. I could whip thee for thinking of it.'

Manasseh says Hota was well whipped by Pastor Tappau ere she was brought to confession,' said Prudence, as if anxious to change the subject of discussion.

Manasseh lifted up his head from the great folio Bible, brought by his father from England, which he was studying. He had not heard what Prudence said, but he looked up at the sound of his name. All present were startled at his wild eyes, his bloodless face. But he was evidently annoyed at the expression of their countenances.

'Why look ye at me in that manner?' asked he. And his manner was anxious and agitated. His mother made haste to speak--

'It was but that Prudence said something that thou hast told her--- that Pastor Tappau defiled his hands by whipping the witch Hota. What evil thought has got hold of thee? Talk to us, and crack not thy skull against the learning of man.'

'It is not the learning of man that I study; it is the Word of God. I would fain know more of the nature of this sin of witchcraft, and whether it be, indeed, the unpardonable sin against the Holy Ghost. At times I feel a creeping influence coming over me, prompting all evil thoughts and unheard-of deeds, and I question within myself, "Is not this the power of witchcraft?" and I sicken, and loathe all that I do or say; and yet some evil creature hath the mastery over me, and I must needs do and say what I loathe and dread. Why wonder you,' mother, that I, of all men, strive to learn the exact nature of witchcraft, and for that end study the Word of God? Have you not seen me when I was, as it were, possessed with a devil?'

He spoke calmly, sadly, but as under deep conviction. His mother rose to comfort him.

'My son,' she said, 'no one ever saw thee do deeds, or heard thee utter words, which any one could say were prompted by devils. We have seen thee, poor lad, with thy wits gone astray for a time; but all thy thoughts sought rather God's will in forbidden places, than lost the clue to them for one moment in hankering after the powers of darkness. Those days are long past; a future lies before thee. Think not of witches, or of being subject to the power of witchcraft. I did evil to speak of it before thee. Let Lois come and sit by thee, and talk to thee.'

Lois went to her cousin, grieved at heart for his depressed state of mind, anxious to soothe and comfort him, and yet recoiling more than ever from the idea of ultimately becoming his wife--an idea to which she saw her aunt reconciling herself unconsciously day by day, as she perceived the English girl's power of soothing and comforting her cousin, even by the very tones of her sweet cooing voice.

He took Lois's hand.

'Let me hold it! It does me good,' said he. 'Ah, Lois, when I am by you, I forget all my troubles--will the day never come when you will listen to the voice that speaks to me continually?'

'I never hear it, Cousin Manasseh,' she said softly; 'but do not think of the voices. Tell me of the land you hope to enclose from the forest--what manner of trees grow on it?' Thus, by simple questions on practical affairs, she led him back, in her unconscious wisdom, to the subjects on which he had always shown strong practical sense. He talked on these, with all due discretion, till the hour for family prayer came round, which was early in those days. It was Manasseh's place to conduct it, as head of the family; a post which his mother had always been anxious to assign to him since her husband's death. He prayed extempore, and tonight his supplications wandered off into wild, unconnected fragments of prayer, which all those kneeling around began, each according to her anxiety for the speaker, to think would never end. Minutes elapsed, and grew to quarters of an hour, and his words only became more emphatic and wilder, praying for himself alone, and laying bare the recesses of his heart. At length his mother rose, and took Lois by the hand; for she had faith in Lois's power over her son, as being akin to that which the shepherd David, playing on his harp, had over king Saul sitting on his throne. She drew her towards him, where he knelt facing into the circle, with his eyes upturned, and the tranced agony of his face depicting the struggle of the troubled soul within.

'Here is Lois,' said Grace, almost tenderly; she would fain go to her chamber.' (Down the girl's face the tears were streaming.) 'Rise, and finish thy prayer in thy closet.'

But at Lois's approach he sprang to his feet--sprang aside.

'Take her away, mother! Lead me not into temptation! She brings me evil and sinful thoughts. She overshadows me, even in the presence of God. She is no angel of light, or she would not do this. She troubles me with the sound of a voice bidding me marry her, even when I am at my prayers. Avaunt! Take her away!'

He would have struck at Lois, if she had not shrunk back, dismayed and affrighted. His mother, although equally dismayed, was not affrighted. She had seen him thus before, and understood the management of his paroxysm.

'Go, Lois! the sight of thee irritates him, as once that of Faith did. Leave him to me!'

And Lois rushed away to her room, and threw herself on her bed, like a panting, hunted creature. Faith came after her slowly and heavily.

'Lois,' said she, 'wilt thou do me a favor? It is not much to ask. Wilt thou arise before daylight, and bear this letter from me to Pastor Nolan's lodgings? I would have done it myself, but mother has bidden me to come to her, and I may be detained until the time when Hota is to be hung; and the letter tells of matters pertaining to life and death. Seek out Pastor Nolan, wherever he may be, and have speech of him after he has read the letter.'

'Cannot Nattee take it?' asked Lois.

'No!' Faith answered fiercely. 'Why should she?'

But Lois did not reply. A quick suspicion darted through Faith's mind, sudden as lightning. It had never entered there before.

'Speak, Lois! I read thy thoughts. Thou would'st fain not be the bearer of this letter?'

'I will take it,' said Lois meekly. 'It concerns life and death, you say?'

'Yes!' said Faith, in quite a different tone of voice. But, after a pause of thought, she added: 'Then, as soon as the house is still, I will write what I have to say, and leave it here on this chest; and thou wilt promise me to take it before the day is fully up, while there is yet time for action.'

'Yes, I promise,' said Lois. And Faith knew enough of her to feel sure that the deed would be done, however reluctantly.

The letter was written--laid on the chest; and, ere day dawned, Lois was astir, Faith watching her from between her half-closed eyelids-- eyelids that had never been fully closed in sleep the livelong night. The instant Lois, cloaked and hooded, left the room, Faith sprang up, and prepared to go to her mother, whom she heard already stirring. Nearly every one in Salem was awake and up on this awful morning, though few were out of doors, as Lois passed along the streets. Here was the hastily-erected gallows, the black shadow of which fell across the street with ghastly significance; now she had to pass the iron- barred gaol, through the unglazed windows of which she heard the fearful cry of a woman, and the sound of many footsteps. On she sped, sick almost to faintness, to the widow woman's where Mr Nolan lodged. He was already up and abroad, gone, his hostess believed, to the gaol. Thither Lois, repeating the words 'for life and for death!' was forced to go. Retracing her steps, she was thankful to see him come out of those dismal portals, rendered more dismal for being in heavy shadow, just as she approached. What his errand had been she knew not; but he looked grave and sad, as she put Faith's letter into his hands, and stood before him quietly waiting until he should read it, and deliver the expected answer. But, instead of opening it, he hid it in his hand, apparently absorbed in thought. At last he spoke aloud, but more to himself than to her--

'My God! and is she, then, to die in this fearful delirium? It must be--can be-- only delirium, that prompts such wild and horrible confessions. Mistress Barclay, I come from the presence of the Indian woman appointed to die. It seems, she considered herself betrayed last evening by her sentence not being respited, even after she had made confession of sin enough to bring down fire from heaven; and, it seems to me, the passionate, impotent anger of this helpless creature has turned to madness, for she appals me by the additional revelations she has made to the keepers during the night--to me this morning. I could almost fancy that she thinks, by deepening the guilt she confesses, to escape this last dread punishment of all; as if, were a tithe of what she says true, one could suffer such a sinner to live! Yet to send her to death in such a state of mad terror! What is to be done?'

'Yet Scripture says that we are not to suffer witches in the land,' said Lois slowly.

'True; I would but ask for a respite, till the prayers of God's people had gone up for His mercy. Some would pray for her, poor wretch as she is. You would, Mistress Barclay, I am sure?' But he said it in a questioning tone.

'I have been praying for her in the night many a time,' said Lois, in a low voice. 'I pray for her in my heart at this moment; I suppose they are bidden to put her out of the land, but I would not have her entirely God-forsaken. But, sir, you have not read my cousin's letter. And she bade me bring back an answer with much urgency.'

Still he delayed. He was thinking of the dreadful confession he came from hearing. If it were true, the beautiful earth was a polluted place, and he almost wished to die, to escape from such pollution, into the white innocence of those who stood in the presence of God.

Suddenly his eyes fell on Lois's pure, grave face, upturned and watching his. Faith in earthly goodness came over his soul in that instant, 'and he blessed her unaware.'

He put his hand on her shoulder, with an action half paternal--- although the difference in their ages was not above a dozen years--- and, bending a little towards her, whispered, half to himself, 'Mistress Barclay, you have done me good.'

'I!' said Lois, half-affrighted; 'I done you good! How?'

'By being what you are. But, perhaps, I should rather thank God, who sent you at the very moment when my soul was so disquieted.'

At this instant, they were aware of Faith standing in front of them, with a countenance of thunder. Her angry look made Lois feel guilty. She had not enough urged the pastor to read his letter, she thought; and it was indignation at this delay in what she had been commissioned to do with the urgency of life or death, that made her cousin lower at her so from beneath her straight black brows. Lois explained how she had not found Mr Nolan at his lodgings, and had bad to follow him to the door of the gaol. But Faith replied, with obdurate contempt--

'Spare thy breath, Cousin Lois! It is easy seeing on what pleasant matters thou and the Pastor Nolan were talking. I marvel not at thy forgetfulness. My mind is changed. Give me back my letter, sir; it was about a poor matter--an old woman's life. And what is that compared to a young girl's love?'

Lois heard but for an instant; did not understand that her cousin, in her jealous anger, could suspect the existence of such a feeling as love between her and Mr Nolan. No imagination as to its possibility had ever entered her mind; she had respected him, almost revered him-- nay, had liked him as the probable husband of Faith. At the thought that her cousin could believe her guilty of such treachery, her grave eyes dilated, and fixed themselves on the flaming countenance of Faith. That serious, unprotesting manner of perfect innocence must have told on her accuser, had it not been that, at the same instant, the latter caught sight of the crimsoned and disturbed countenance of the pastor, who felt the veil rent off the unconscious secret of his heart. Faith snatched her letter out of his hands, and said--

'Let the witch hang! What care I? She has done harm enough with her charms and her sorcery on Pastor Tappau's girls. Let her die, and let all other witches look to themselves; for there be many kinds of witchcraft abroad. Cousin Lois, thou wilt like best to stop with Pastor Nolan, or I would pray thee to come back with me to breakfast.'

Lois was not to be daunted by jealous sarcasm. She held out her hand to Pastor Nolan, determined to take no heed of her cousin's mad words, but to bid him farewell in her accustomed manner. He hesitated before taking it; and, when he did, it was with a convulsive squeeze that almost made her start. Faith waited and watched all, with set lips and vengeful eyes. She bade no farewell; she spoke no word; but, grasping Lois tightly by the back of the arm, she almost drove her before her down the street till they reached their home.

The arrangement for the morning was this: Grace Hickson and her son Manasseh were to be present at the hanging of the first witch executed in Salem, as pious and godly heads of a family. All the other members were strictly forbidden to stir out, until such time as the low- tolling bell announced that all was over in this world for Hota, the Indian witch. When the execution was ended, there was to be a solemn prayer-meeting of all the inhabitants of Salem; ministers had come from a distance to aid by the efficacy of their prayers in these efforts to purge the land of the devil and his servants. There was reason to think that the great old meeting-house would be crowded; and, when Faith and Lois reached home, Grace Hickson was giving her directions to Prudence, urging her to be ready for an early start to that place. The stern old woman was troubled in her mind at the anticipation of the sight she was to see, before many minutes were over, and spoke in a more hurried and incoherent manner than was her wont. She was dressed in her Sunday best; but her face was very grey and colorless, and she seemed afraid to cease speaking about household affairs, for fear she should have time to think. Manasseh stood by her, perfectly, rigidly still; he also was in his Sunday clothes. His face, too, was paler than its wont; but it wore a kind of absent, rapt expression, almost like that of a man who sees a vision. As Faith entered, still holding Lois in her fierce grasp, Manasseh started and smiled, but still dreamily. His manner was so peculiar that even his mother stayed her talking to observe him more closely; he was in that state of excitement which usually ended in what his mother and certain of her friends esteemed a prophetic revelation. He began to speak, at first very low, and then his voice increased in power.

'How beautiful is the land of Beulah, far over the sea, beyond the mountains! Thither the angels carry her, lying back in their arms like one fainting. They shall kiss away the black circle of death, and lay her down at the feet of the Lamb. I hear her pleading there for those on earth who consented to her death. O Lois! pray also for me, pray for me, miserable!'

When he uttered his cousin's name all their eyes turned towards her. It was to her that his vision related! She stood among them, amazed, awe-stricken, but not like one affrighted or dismayed. She was the first to speak--

'Dear friends, do not think of me; his words may or may not be true. I am in God's hands all the same, whether he have the gift of prophecy or not. Besides, hear you not that I end where all would fain end? Think of him, and of his needs! Such times as these always leave him exhausted and weary, and he comes out of them.'

And she busied herself in cares for his refreshment, aiding her aunt's trembling hands to set before him the requisite food, as he now sat tired and bewildered, gathering together with difficulty his scattered senses.

Prudence did all she could to assist and speed their departure. But Faith stood apart, watching in silence with her passionate, angry eyes.

As soon as they had set out on their solemn, fatal errand, Faith left the room. She had not tasted food or touched drink. Indeed, they all felt sick at heart. The moment her sister had gone upstairs, Prudence sprang to the settle on which Lois had thrown down her cloak and hood--

'Lend me your muffles and mantle, Cousin Lois. I never yet saw a woman hanged, and I see not why I should not go. I will stand on the edge of the crowd; no one will know me, and I will be home long before my mother.'

'No!' said Lois, 'that may not be. My aunt would be sore displeased. I wonder at you, Prudence, seeking to witness such a sight.' And as she spoke she held fast her cloak, which Prudence vehemently struggled for.

Faith returned, brought back possibly by the sound of the struggle. She smiled-- a deadly smile.

'Give it up, Prudence. Strive no more with her. She has bought success in this world, and we are but her slaves.'

'Oh, Faith' said Lois, relinquishing her hold of the cloak, and turning round with passionate reproach in her look and voice, 'what have I done that you should speak so of me: you, that I have loved as I think one loves a sister?'

Prudence did not lose her opportunity, but hastily arrayed herself in the mantle, which was too large for her, and which she had, therefore, considered as well adapted for concealment; but, as she went towards the door, her feet became entangled in the unusual length, and she fell, bruising her arm pretty sharply.

'Take care, another time, how you meddle with a witch's things,' said Faith, as one scarcely believing her own words, but at enmity with all the world in her bitter jealousy of heart. Prudence rubbed her arm, and looked stealthily at Lois.

'Witch Lois! Witch Lois!' said she at last, softly, pulling a childish face of spite at her.

'Oh, hush, Prudence! Do not bandy such terrible words! Let me look at thine arm! I am sorry for thy hurt; only glad that it has kept thee from disobeying thy mother.'

'Away, away!' said Prudence, springing from her. 'I am afeared of her in very truth, Faith. Keep between me and the witch, or I will throw a stool at her.'

Faith smiled--it was a bad and wicked smile--but she did not stir to calm the fears she had called up in her young sister, just at this moment, the bell began to toll. Hota, the Indian witch, was dead. Lois covered her face with her hands. Even Faith went a deadlier pale than she had been, and said, sighing, 'Poor Hota! But death is best.'

Prudence alone seemed unmoved by any thoughts connected with the solemn, monotonous sound. Her only consideration was, that now she might go out into the street and see the sights, and hear the news, and escape from the terror which she felt at the presence of her cousin. She flew upstairs to find her own mantle, ran down again, and past Lois, before the English girl had finished her prayer, and was speedily mingled among the crowd going to the meeting-house. There also Faith and Lois came in due course of rime, but separately, not together. Faith so evidently avoided Lois that she, humbled and grieved, could not force her company upon her cousin, but loitered a little behind---the quiet tears stealing down her face, shed for the many causes that had occurred this morning.

The meeting-house was full to suffocation; and, as it sometimes happens on such occasions, the greatest crowd was close about the doors, from the fact that few saw, on their first entrance, where there might be possible spaces into which they could wedge themselves. Yet they were impatient of any arrivals from the outside, and pushed and hustled Faith, and after her Lois, till the two were forced on to a conspicuous place in the very centre of the building, where there was no chance of a seat, but still space to stand in. Several stood around, the pulpit being in the middle, and already occupied by two ministers in Geneva bands and gowns, while other ministers, similarly attired, stood holding on to it, almost as if they were giving support instead of receiving it. Grace Hickson and her son sat decorously in their own pew, thereby showing that they had arrived early from the execution. You might almost have traced out the number of those who had been at the hanging of the Indian witch, by the expression of their countenances. They were awe-stricken into terrible repose; while the crowd pouring in, still pouring in, of those who had not attended the execution, looked all restless, and excited, and fierce. A buzz went round the meeting that the stranger minister who stood along with Pastor Tappau in the pulpit was no other than Dr Cotton Mather himself, come all the way from Boston to assist in purging Salem of witches.

And now Pastor Tappau began his prayer, extempore, as was the custom. His words were wild and incoherent, as might be expected from a man who had just been consenting to the bloody death of one who was, but a few days ago, a member of his own family; violent and passionate, as was to be looked for in the father of children, whom he believed to suffer so fearfully from the crime he would denounce before the Lord. He sat down at length from pure exhaustion. Then Dr Cotton Mather stood forward; he did not utter more than a few words of prayer, calm in comparison with what had gone before, and then he went on to address the great crowd before him in a quiet, argumentative way, but arranging what he had to say with something of the same kind of skill which Antony used in his speech to the Romans after C¾sar's murder. Some of Dr Mather's words have been preserved to us, as he afterwards wrote them down in one of his works. Speaking of those 'unbelieving Sadducees' who doubted the existence of such a crime, he said: 'Instead of their apish shouts and jeers at blessed Scripture, and histories which have such undoubted confirmation as that no man that has breeding enough to regard the common laws of human society will offer to doubt of them, it becomes us rather to adore the goodness of God, who from the mouths of babes and sucklings has ordained truth, and by the means of the sore-afflicted children of your godly pastor, has revealed the fact that the devils have with most horrid operations broken in upon your neighborhood. Let us beseech Him that their power may be restrained, and that they go not so far in their evil machinations as they did but four years ago in the city of Boston, where I was the humble means, under God, of loosing from the power of Satan the four children of that religious and blessed man, Mr Goodwin. These four babes of grace were bewitched by an Irish witch; there is no end of the narration of the torments they had to submit to. At one time they would bark like dogs, at another purr like cats; yea, they would fly like geese, and be carried with an incredible swiftness, having but just their toes now and then upon the ground, sometimes not once in twenty feet, and their arms waved like those of a bird. Yet, at other times, by the hellish devices of the woman who had bewitched them, they could not stir without limping; for, by means of an invisible chain, she hampered their limbs, or sometimes, by means of a noose, almost choked them. One, in special, was subjected by this woman of Satan to such heat as of an oven, that I myself have seen the sweat drop from off her, while all around were moderately cold and well at ease. But not to trouble you with more of my stories, I will go on to prove that it was Satan himself that held power over her. For a very remarkable thing it was, that she was not permitted by that evil spirit to read any godly or religious book, speaking the truth as it is in Jesus. She could read Popish books well enough, while both sight and speech seemed to fail her, when I gave her the Assembly's Catechism. Again, she was fond of that prelatical Book of Common Prayer, which is but the Roman mass-book in an English and ungodly shape. In the midst of her sufferings, if one put the Prayer-book into her hands, it relieved her. Yet, mark you, she could never be brought to read the Lord's Prayer, whatever book she met with it in, proving thereby distinctly that she was in league with the devil. I took her into my own house, that I, even as Dr Martin Luther did, might wrestle with the devil, and have my fling at him. But, when I called my household to prayer, the devils that possessed her caused her to whistle, and sing, and yell in a discordant and hellish fashion.'

At this very instant a shrill, clear whistle pierced all ears. Dr Mather stopped for a moment--

'Satan is among you!' he cried. 'Look to yourselves!' And he prayed with fervor, as if against a present and threatening enemy; but no one heeded him. Whence came that ominous, unearthly whistle? Every man watched his neighbor. Again the whistle, out of their very midst! And then a bustle in a corner of the building; three or four people stirring, without any cause immediately perceptible to those at a distance; the movement spread; and, directly after, a passage even in that dense mass of people was cleared for two men, who bore forwards Prudence Hickson, lying rigid as a log of wood, in the convulsive position of one who suffered from an epileptic fit. They laid her down among the ministers who were gathered round the pulpit. Her mother came to her, sending up a wailing cry at the sight of her distorted child. Dr Mather came down from the pulpit and stood over her, exorcising the devil in possession, as one accustomed to such scenes. The crowd pressed forward in mute horror. At length her rigidity of form and feature gave way, and she was terribly convulsed--torn by the devil, as they called it. By and by, the violence of the attack was over, and the spectators began to breathe once more; though still the former horror brooded over them, and they listened as if for the sudden ominous whistle again, and glanced fearfully around, as if Satan were at their backs picking out his next victim.

Meanwhile, Dr Mather, Pastor Tappau, and one or two others, were exhorting Prudence to reveal, if she could, the name of the person, the witch, who, by influence over Satan, had subjected the child to such torture as that which they had just witnessed. They bade her speak in the name of the Lord. She whispered a name in the low voice of exhaustion. None of the congregation could hear what it was. But the Pastor Tappau, when he heard it drew back in dismay, while Dr Mather, knowing not to whom the name belonged, cried out, in a clear, cold voice--

Know ye one Lois Barclay; for it is she who bath bewitched this poor child?'

The answer was given rather by action than by word, although a low murmur went up from many. But all fell back, as far as falling back in such a crowd was possible, from Lois Barclay, where she stood--and looked on her with surprise and horror. A space of some feet, where no possibility of space had seemed to be not a minute before, left Lois standing alone, with every eye fixed upon her in hatred and dread. She stood like one speechless, tongue-tied, as if in a dream. She a witch! accursed as witches were in the sight of God and man! Her smooth, healthy face became contracted into shrivel and pallor; but she uttered not a word, only looked at Dr Mather with her dilated terrified eyes.

Some one said, 'She is of the household of Grace Hickson, a God- fearing women.' Lois did not know if the words were in her favor or not. She did not think about them, even; they told less on her than on any person present. She a witch! and the silver glittering Avon, and the drowning woman she had seen in her childhood at Barford--at home in England--was before her, and her eyes fell before her doom. There was some commotion--some rustling of papers; the magistrates of the town were drawing near the pulpit and consulting with the ministers. Dr Mather spoke again--

'The Indian woman, who was hung this morning, named certain people, whom she deposed to have seen at the horrible meetings for the worship of Satan; but there is no name of Lois Barclay down upon the paper, although we are stricken at the sight of the names of some'--

An interruption--a consultation. Again Dr Mather spoke--

'Bring the accused witch, Lois Barclay, near to this poor suffering child of Christ.'

They rushed forward to force Lois to the place where Prudence lay. But Lois walked forward of herself--

'Prudence,' she said, in such a sweet, touching voice, that, long afterwards, those who heard it that day spoke of it to their children, 'have I ever said an unkind word to you, much less done you an ill rum? Speak, dear child! You did not know what you said just now, did you?'

But Prudence writhed away from her approach, and screamed out, as if stricken with fresh agony--

'Take her away! take her away! Witch Lois! Witch Lois, who threw me down only this morning, and turned my arm black and blue.' And she bared her arm, as if in confirmation of her words. It was sorely bruised.

'I was not near you, Prudence!' said Lois sadly. But that was only reckoned fresh evidence of her diabolical power.

Lois's brain began to get bewildered. 'Witch Lois'! She a witch, abhorred of all men! yet she would try to think, and make one more effort.

'Aunt Hickson,' she said, and Grace came forwards. 'Am I a witch, Aunt Hickson?' she asked; for her aunt, stern, harsh, unloving as she might be, was truth itself, and Lois thought--so near to delirium had she come--if her aunt condemned her, it was possible she might indeed be a witch.

Grace Hickson faced her unwillingly.

'It is a stain upon our family for ever,' was the thought in her mind.

'It is for God to judge whether thou art a witch or not. Not for me. I

'Alas, alas!' moaned Lois; for she had looked at Faith, and learnt that no good word was to be expected from her gloomy face and averted eyes. The meeting-house was full of eager voices, repressed, out of reverence for the place, into tones of earnest murmuring that seemed to fill the air with gathering sounds of anger; and those who had first fallen back from the place where Lois stood were now pressing forwards and round about her, ready to seize the young friendless girl, and bear her off to prison. Those who might have been, who ought to have been, her friends, were either averse or indifferent to her; though only Prudence made any open outcry upon her. That evil child cried out perpetually that Lois had cast a devilish spell upon her, and bade them keep the witch away from her; and, indeed, Prudence was strangely convulsed, when once or twice Lois's perplexed and wistful eyes were turned in her direction. Here and there, girls, women, tittering strange cries, and apparently suffering from the same kind of convulsive fit as that which had attacked Prudence, were centres of a group of agitated friends, who muttered much and savagely of witchcraft, and the list which had been taken down only the night before from Hota's own lips. They demanded to have it made public, and objected to the slow forms of the law. Others, not so much or so immediately interested in the sufferers, were kneeling around, and praying aloud for themselves and their own safety, until the excitement should be so much quelled as to enable Dr Cotton Mather to be again heard in prayer and exhortation.

And where was Manasseh? What said he? You must remember that the stir of the outcry, the accusation, the appeals of the accused, all seemed to go on at once, amid die buzz and din of the people who had come to worship God, but remained to judge and upbraid their fellow-creature. Tin now, Lois had only caught a glimpse of Manasseh, who was apparently trying to push forwards, but whom his mother was holding back with word and action, as Lois knew she would hold him back; for it was not for the first time that she was made aware how carefully her aunt had always shrouded his decent reputation among his fellow- citizens from the least suspicion of his seasons of excitement and incipient insanity. On such days, when he himself imagined that he heard prophetic voices and saw prophetic visions, his mother would do much to prevent any besides his own family from seeing Mm; and now Lois, by a process swifter than reasoning, felt certain, from her one look at his face when she saw it, colorless and deformed by intensity of expression, among a number of others, all simply ruddy and angry, that he was in such a state that his mother would in vain do her utmost to prevent his making himself conspicuous. Whatever force or argument Grace used, it was of no avail. In another moment, he was by Lois's side, stammering with excitement, and giving vague testimony, which would have been of little value in a calm court of justice, and was only oil to the smoldering fire of that audience.

'Away with her to gaol!' 'Seek out the witches!' 'The sin has spread into all households!' 'Satan is in the very midst of us!' 'Strike and spare not!' In vain Dr Cotton Mather raised his voice in loud prayers, in which he assumed the guilt of the accused girl; no one listened, all were anxious to secure Lois, as if they feared she would vanish from before their very eyes: she, white, trembling, standing quite still in the tight grasp of strange, fierce men, her dilated eyes only wandering a little now and then in search of some pitiful face---some pitiful face that, among all those hundreds, was not to be found. While some fetched cords to bind her, and others, by low questions, suggested new accusations to the distempered brain of Prudence, Manasseh obtained a hearing once more. Addressing Dr Cotton Mather, he said, evidently anxious to make clear some new argument that had just suggested itself to him: 'Sir, in this matter, be she witch or not, the end has been foreshown to me by the spirit of prophecy. Now, reverend sir, if the event be known to the spirit, it must have been foredoomed in the counsels of God. If so, why punish her for doing that in which she had no free-will?'

'Young man,' said Dr Mather, bending down from the pulpit and looking very severely upon Manasseh, 'Take care! you arc trenching on blasphemy.'

'I do not care. I say it again. Either Lois Barclay is a witch, or she is not. If she is, it has been foredoomed for her, for I have seen a vision of her death as a condemned witch for many months past--and the voice has told me there was but one escape for her--Lois--the voice you know'--In his excitement he began to wander a little; but it was touching to see how conscious he was, that by giving way he would lose the thread of the logical argument by which he hoped to prove that Lois ought not to be punished, and with what an effort he wrenched his imagination away from the old ideas, and strove to concentrate all his mind upon the plea that, if Lois was a witch, it had been shown him by prophecy: and, if there was prophecy, there must be foreknowledge; if foreknowledge, no freedom; if no freedom, no exercise of free-will; and, therefore, that Lois was not justly amenable to punishment.

On he went, plunging into heresy, caring not--growing more and more passionate every instant, but directing his passion into keen argument, desperate sarcasm, instead of allowing it to excite his imagination. Even Dr Mather felt himself on the point of being worsted in the very presence of this congregation, who, but a short half-hour ago, looked upon him as all but infallible. Keep a good heart, Cotton Mather! your opponent's eye begins to glare and flicker with a terrible, yet uncertain, light--his speech grows less coherent, and his arguments are mixed up with wild glimpses at wilder revelations made to himself alone. He has touched on the limits--he has entered the borders--of blasphemy; and, with an awful cry of horror and reprobation, the congregation rise up, as one man, against the blasphemer. Dr Mather smiled a grim smile; and the people were ready to stone Manasseh, who went on, regardless, talking and raving.

'Stay, stay!' said Grace Hickson--all the decent family shame which prompted her to conceal the mysterious misfortune of her only son from public knowledge done away with by the sense of the immediate danger to his life. 'Touch him not! He knows not what he is saying. The fit is upon him. I tell you the truth before God. My son, my only son, is mad.'

They stood aghast at the intelligence. The grave young citizen, who had silently taken his part in life close by them in their daily lives--not mixing much with them, it was true, but looked up to, perhaps, all the more--the student of abstruse books on theology, fit to converse with the most learned ministers that ever came about those parts--was he the same with the man now pouring out wild words to Lois the witch, as if he and she were the only two present? A solution of it all occurred to them. He was another victim. Great was the power of Satan! Through the arts of the devil, that white statue of a girl had mastered the soul of Manasseh Hickson. SO the word spread from mouth to mouth. And Grace heard it. It seemed a healing balsam for her shame. With wilful, dishonest blindness, she would not see--not even in her secret heart would she acknowledge--that Manasseh had been strange, and moody, and violent long before the English girl had reached Salem. She even found some specious reason for his attempt at suicide long ago. He was recovering from a fever--and though tolerably well in health, the delirium had not finally left him. But since Lois came, how headstrong he had been at times! how unreasonable! how moody! What a strange delusion was that which he was under, of being bidden by some voice to marry her! How he followed her about, and clung to her, as under some compulsion of affection! And over all reigned the idea that, if he were indeed suffering from being bewitched, he was not mad, and might again assume the honorable position he had held in the congregation and in the town, when the spell by which he was held was destroyed. So Grace yielded to the notion herself, and encouraged it in others, that Lois Barclay had bewitched both Manasseh and Prudence. And the consequence of this belief was, that Lois was to be tried, with little chance in her favor, to see whether she was a witch or no; and if a witch, whether she would confess, implicate others, repent, and live a life of bitter shame, avoided by all men, and cruelly treated by most; or die, impenitent, hardened, denying her crime upon the gallows.

And so they dragged Lois away from the congregation of Christians to the gaol, to await her trial. I say 'dragged her': because, although she was docile enough to have followed them whither they would, she was now so faint as to require extraneous force--poor Lois! who should have been carried and tended lovingly in her state of exhaustion; but, instead, was so detested by the multitude, who looked upon her as an accomplice of Satan in all his evil doings, that they cared no more how they treated her than a careless boy minds how he handles the toad that he is going to throw over the wall.

When Lois came to her full senses, she found herself lying on a short, hard bed in a dark, square room, which she at once knew must be a part of the city gaol. It was about eight feet square; it had stone walls on every side, and a grated opening high above her head, letting in all the light and air that could enter through about a square foot of aperture. It was so lonely, so dark to that poor girl, when she came slowly and painfully out of her long faint. She did so want human help in that struggle which always supervenes after a swoon; when the effort is to clutch at life, and the effort seems too much for the will. She did not at first understand where she was, did not understand how she came to be there; nor did she care to understand. Her physical instinct was to lie still and let the hurrying pulses have time to calm. So she shut her eyes once more. Slowly, slowly the recollection of the scene in the meeting-house shaped itself into a kind of picture before her. She saw within her eyelids, as it were, that sea of loathing faces all turned towards her, as towards something unclean and hateful. And you must remember, you who in the nineteenth century read this account, that witchcraft was a real terrible sin to her, Lois Barclay, two hundred years ago. The look on their faces, stamped on heart and brain, excited in her a sort of strange sympathy. Could it, O God!--could it be true, that Satan had obtained the terrific power over her and her will of which she had heard and read? Could she indeed be possessed by a demon and be indeed a witch, and yet till now have been unconscious of it? And her excited imagination recalled, with singular vividness, all she had ever heard on the subject--the horrible midnight sacrament, the very presence and power of Satan. Then, remembering every angry thought against her neighbor, against the impertinences of Prudence, against the overbearing authority of her aunt, against the persevering crazy suit of Manasseh, her indignation--only that morning, but such ages off in real time--at Faith's injustice: oh, could such evil thoughts have had devilish power given to them by the father of evil, and, all unconsciously to herself, have gone forth as active curses in die world? And so the ideas went on careering wildly through the poor girl's brain, the girl thrown inward upon herself. At length, the sting of her imagination forced her to start up impatiently. What was this? A weight of iron on her legs--a weight stated afterwards, by the gaoler of Salem prison, to have been 'not more than eight pounds.' It was well for Lois it was a tangible ill, bringing her back from the wild, illimitable desert in which her imagination was wandering. She took hold of the iron, and saw her torn stocking, her bruised ankle, and began to cry pitifully, out of strange compassion with herself. They feared, then, that even in that cell she would find a way to escape! Why, the utter, ridiculous impossibility of the thing convinced her of her own innocence and ignorance of all supernatural power; and the heavy iron brought her strangely round from the delusions that seemed to be gathering about her.

No! she never could fly out of that deep dungeon; there was no escape, natural or supernatural, for her, unless by man's mercy. And what was man's mercy in such times of panic? Lois knew that it was nothing; instinct, more than reason, taught her that panic calls out cowardice, and cowardice cruelty. Yet she cried, cried freely, and for the first time, when she found herself ironed and chained. It seemed so cruel, so much as if her fellow-creatures had really learnt to hate and dread her--her, who had had a few angry thoughts, which God forgive! but whose thoughts had never gone into words, far less into actions. Why, even now she could love all the household at home, if they would but let her; yes, even yet, though she felt that it was the open accusation of Prudence and the withheld justifications of her aunt and Faith that had brought her to her present strait. Would they ever come and see her? Would kinder thoughts of her--who had shared their daily bread for months and months--bring them to see her, and ask her whether it were really she who had brought on the illness of Prudence, the derangement of Manasseh's mind? No one came. Bread and water were pushed in by some one, who hastily locked and unlocked the door, and cared not to see if he put them within his prisoner's reach, or perhaps thought that that physical fact mattered little to a witch. It was long before Lois could reach them; and she had something of the natural hunger of youth left in her still, which prompted her, lying her length on the floor, to weary herself with efforts to obtain the bread. After she had eaten some of it, the day began to wane, and she thought she would lay her down and try to sleep. But before she did so, the gaoler heard her singing the Evening Hymn--

'Glory to Thee, my God, this night,

For all the blessings of the light!'

And a dull thought came into his dull mind, that she was thankful for few blessings, if she could tune up her voice to sing praises after this day of what, if she were a witch, was shameful detection in abominable practices, and if not-- Well, his mind stopped short at this point in his wondering contemplation. Lois knelt down and said the Lord's Prayer, pausing just a little before one clause, that she might be sure that in her heart of hearts she did forgive. Then she looked at her ankle, and the tears came into her eyes once again; but not so much because she was hurt, as because men must have hated her so bitterly before they could have treated her thus. Then she lay down and fell asleep.

The next day, she was led before Mr Hathorn and Mr Curwin, justices of Salem, to be accused legally and publicly of witchcraft. Others were with her, under the same charge. And when the prisoners were brought in, they were cried out at by the abhorrent crowd. The two Tappaus, Prudence, and one or two other girls of the same age were there, in the character of victims of the spells of the accused. The prisoners were placed about seven or eight feet from the justices, and the accusers between the justices and them; the former were then ordered to stand right before the justices. All this Lois did at their bidding, with something of the wondering docility of a child, but not with any hope of softening the hard, stony look of detestation that was on all the countenances around her, save those that were distorted by more passionate anger. Then an officer was bidden to hold each of her hands, and justice Hathorn bade her keep her eyes continually fixed on him, for this reason--which, however, was not told to her-- lest, if she looked on Prudence, the girl might either fall into a fit, or cry out that she was suddenly or violently hurt. If any heart could have been touched in that cruel multitude, they would have felt some compassion for the sweet young face of the English girl, trying so meekly to do all that she was ordered, her face quite white, yet so full of sad gentleness, her grey eyes, a little dilated by the very solemnity of her position, fixed with the intent look of innocent maidenhood on the stem face of justice Hathorn. And thus they stood in silence, one breathless minute. Then they were bidden to say the Lord's Prayer. Lois went through it as if alone in her cell; but, as she had done alone in her cell the night before, she made a little pause, before the prayer to be forgiven as she forgave. And at this instant of hesitation--as if they had been on the watch for it--they all cried out upon her for a witch; and, when the clamor ended, the justices bade Prudence Hickson come forward. Then Lois turned a little to one side, wishing to see at least one familiar face; but, when her eyes fell upon Prudence, the girl stood stock-still, and answered no questions, nor spoke a word, and the justices declared that she was struck dumb by witchcraft. Then some behind took Prudence under the arms, and would have forced her forwards to touch Lois, possibly esteeming that as a cure for her being bewitched. But Prudence had hardly been made to take three steps, before she struggled out of their arms and fell down writhing, as in a fit, calling out with shrieks, and entreating Lois to help her, and save her from her torment. Then all the girls began 'to tumble down like swine' (to use the words of an eye-witness) and to cry out upon Lois and her fellow- prisoners. These last were now ordered to stand with their hands stretched out, it being imagined that, if the bodies of the witches were arranged in the form of a cross, they would lose their evil power. By and by, Lois felt her strength going, from the unwonted fatigue of such a position, which she had borne patiently until the pain and weariness had forced both tears and sweat down her face; and she asked, in a low, plaintive voice, if she might not rest her head for a few moments against the wooden partition. But justice Hathorn told her she had strength enough to torment others, and should have strength enough to stand. She sighed a little, and bore on, the clamour against her and the other accused increasing every moment; the only way she could keep herself from utterly losing consciousness was by distracting herself from present pain and danger, and saying to herself verses of the Psalms as she could remember them, expressive of trust in God. At length, she was ordered back to gaol, and dimly understood that she and others were sentenced to be hanged for witchcraft. Many people now looked eagerly at Lois, to see if she would weep at this doom. If she had had strength to cry, it might--it was just possible that it might--have been considered a plea in her favor, for witches could not shed tears; but she was too exhausted and dead. All she wanted was to lie down once more on her prison-bed, out of the reach of men's cries of abhorrence, and out of shot of their cruel eyes. So they led her back to prison, speechless and tearless.

But rest gave her back her power of thought and suffering. Was it indeed true that she was to die? She, Lois Barclay, only eighteen, so well, so young, so full of love and hope as she had been, till but these few days past! What would they think of it at home--real, dear home at Barford, in England? There they had loved her; there she had gone about singing and rejoicing, all the day long, in the pleasant meadows by the Avon side. Oh, why did father and mother die, and leave her their bidding to come her to this cruel New England shore, where no one had wanted her, no one had cared for her, and where now they were going to put her to a shameful death as a witch? And there would be no one to send kindly messages by, to those she should never see more. Never more! Young Lucy was living, and joyful--probably thinking of her, and of his declared intention of coming to fetch her home to be his wife this very spring. Possibly he had forgotten her; no one knew. A week before, she would have been indignant at her own distrust in thinking for a minute that he could forget. Now, she doubted all men's goodness for a time; for those around her were deadly, and cruel, and relentless.

Then she turned round, and beat herself with angry blows (to speak in images) for ever doubting her lover. Oh! if she were but with him! Oh! if she might but be with him! He would not let her die, but would hide her in his bosom from the wrath of this people, and carry her back to the old home at Barford. And he might even now be sailing on the wide blue sea, coming nearer, nearer every moment, and yet be too late after all.

So the thoughts chased each other through her head all that feverish night, till she clung almost deliriously to life, and wildly prayed that she might not die; at least, not just yet, and she so young!

Pastor Tappau and certain elders roused her up from a heavy sleep, late on the morning of the following day. All night long, she had trembled and cried, till morning light had come peering in through the square grating up above. It soothed her, and she fell asleep, to be awakened, as I have said, by Pastor Tappau.

'Arise!' said he, scrupling to touch her, from his superstitious idea of her evil powers. 'It is noonday.'

'Where am I?' said she, bewildered at this unusual wakening and the array of severe faces, all gazing upon her with reprobation.

'You are in Salem gaol, condemned for a witch.'

'Alas! I had forgotten for an instant,' said she, dropping her head upon her breast.

'She has been out on a devilish ride all night long, doubtless, and is weary and perplexed this morning,' whispered one in so low a voice that he did not think she could hear; but she lifted up her eyes, and looked at him, with mute reproach.

'We are come,' said Pastor Tappau, 'to exhort you to confess your great and manifold sin.'

'My great and manifold sin!' repeated Lois to herself, shaking her head.

'Yea, your sin of witchcraft. If you will confess, there may yet be balm in Gilead.'

One of the elders, struck with pity at the young girl's wan, shrunken look, said that if she confessed and repented, and did penance, possibly her life might yet be spared.

A sudden flash of light came into her sunk, dulled eye. Might she yet live? Was it in her power? Why, no one knew how soon Hugh Lucy might be here, to take her away for ever into the peace of a new home! Life! Oh, then, all hope was not over--perhaps she might still live, and not die. Yet the truth came once more out of her lips, almost without exercise of her will.

'I am not a witch,' she said.

Then Pastor Tappau blindfolded her, all unresisting, but with languid wonder in her heart as to what was to come next. She heard people enter the dungeon softly, and heard whispering voices; then her hands were lifted up and made to touch some one near, and in an instant she heard a noise of struggling, and the well-known voice of Prudence shrieking out in one of her hysterical fits, and screaming to be taken away and out of that place. It seemed to Lois as if some of her judges must have doubted of her guilt, and demanded yet another test.

She sat down heavily on her bed, thinking she must be in a horrible dream, so compassed about with dangers and enemies did she seem. Those in the dungeon--and, by the oppression of the air, she perceived that there were many--kept on eager talking in low voices. She did not try to make out the sense of the fragments of sentences that reached her dulled brain, till, all at once, a word or two made her understand they were discussing the desirableness of applying the whip or the torture to make her confess, and reveal by what means the spell she had cast upon those whom she had bewitched could be dissolved. A thrill of affright ran through her; and she cried out beseechingly--

'I beg you, sirs, for God's mercy sake, that you do not use such awful means. I may say anything--nay, I may accuse any one--if I am subjected to such torment as I have heard tell about. For I am but a young girl, and not very brave, or very good, as some are.'

It touched the hearts of one or two to see her standing there; the tears streaming down from below the coarse handkerchief, tightly bound over her eyes; the clanking chain fastening the heavy weight to the slight ankle; the two hands held together, as if to keep down a convulsive motion.

'Look!' said one of these. 'She is weeping. They say no witch can weep tears.'

But another scoffed at this test, and bade the first remember how those of her own family, the Hicksons even, bore witness against her.

Once more, she was bidden to confess. The charges, esteemed by all men (as they said) to have been proven against her, were read over to her, with all the testimony borne against her in proof thereof. They told her that, considering the godly family to which she belonged, it had been decided by the magistrates and ministers of Salem that she should have her life spared, if she would own her guilt, make reparation, and submit to penance; but that, if not, she and others convicted of witchcraft along with her, were to be hung in Salem market-place on the next Thursday morning (Thursday being market-day). And when they had thus spoken, they waited silently for her answer. It was a minute or two before she spoke. She had sat down again upon the bed meanwhile; for indeed she was very weak. She asked, 'May I have this handkerchief unbound from my eyes; for indeed, sirs, it hurts me?'

The occasion for which she was blindfolded being over, the bandage was taken off, and she was allowed to see. She looked pitifully at the stern faces around her, in grim suspense as to what her answer would be. Then she spoke--

'Sirs, I must choose death with a quiet conscience rather than life to be gained by a lie. I am not a witch. I know not hardly what you mean, when you say I am. I have done many, many things very wrong in my life; but I think God will forgive me them for my Savior's sake.'

'Take not His name on your wicked lips,' said Pastor Tappau, enraged at her resolution of not confessing, and scarcely able to keep himself from striking her. She saw the desire he had, and shrank away in timid fear. Then justice Hathorn solemnly read the legal condemnation of Lois Barclay to death by hanging, as a convicted witch. She murmured something which nobody heard fully, but which sounded like a prayer for pity and compassion on her tender years and friendless estate. Then they left her to all the horrors of that solitary, loathsome dungeon, and the strange terror of approaching death.

Outside the prison-walls, the dread of the witches, and the excitement against witchcraft, grew with fearful rapidity. Numbers of women, and men, too, were accused, no matter what their station of life and their former character had been. On the other side, it is alleged that upwards of fifty persons were grievously vexed by the devil, and those to whom he had imparted of his power for vile and wicked considerations. How much of malice--distinct, unmistakable, personal malice--was mixed up with these accusations, no one can now tell. The dire statistics of this time tell us, that fifty-five escaped death by confessing themselves guilty; one hundred and fifty were in prison; more than two hundred accused; and upwards of twenty suffered death, among whom was the minister I have called Nolan, who was traditionally esteemed to have suffered through hatred of his co-pastor. One old man, scorning the accusation, and refusing to plead at his trial, was, according to the law, pressed to death for his contumacy. Nay, even dogs were accused of witchcraft, suffered the legal penalties, and are recorded among the subjects of capital punishment. One young man found means to effect his mother's escape from confinement, fled with her on horseback, and secreted her in the Blueberry Swamp, not far from Taplay's Brook, in the Great Pasture; he concealed her here in a wigwam which he built for her shelter, provided her with food and clothing, and comforted and sustained her, until after the delusion had passed away. The poor creature must, however, have suffered dreadfully; for one of her arms was fractured in the all but desperate effort of getting her out of prison.

But there was no one to try and save Lois. Grace Hickson would fain have ignored her altogether. Such a taint did witchcraft bring upon a whole family, that generations of blameless life were not at that day esteemed sufficient to wash it out. Besides, you must remember that Grace, along with most people of her time, believed most firmly in the reality of the crime of witchcraft. Poor, forsaken Lois believed in it herself; and it added to her terror, for the gaoler, in an unusually communicative mood, told her that nearly every cell was now full of witches, and it was possible he might have to put one, if more came, in with her. Lois knew that she was no witch herself; but not the less did she believe that the crime was abroad, and largely shared in by evil-minded persons who had chosen to give up their souls to Satan; and she shuddered with terror at what the gaoler said, and would have asked him to spare her this companionship, if it were possible. But, somehow, her senses were leaving her; and she could not remember the right words in which to form her request, until he had left the place.

The only person who yearned after Lois--who would have befriended her if he could--was Manasseh, poor, made Manasseh. But he was so wild and outrageous in his talk, that it was all his mother could do to keep his state concealed from public observation. She had for this purpose given him a sleeping potion; and, while he lay heavy and inert under the influence of the poppy-tea, his mother bound him with cords to the ponderous, antique bed in which he slept. She looked brokenhearted, while she did this office and thus acknowledged the degradation of her first-born--him of whom she had ever been so proud.

Late that evening, Grace Hickson stood in Lois's cell, hooded and cloaked up to her eyes. Lois was sitting quite still, playing idly with a bit of string which one of the magistrates had dropped out of his pocket that morning. Her aunt was standing by her for an instant or two in silence, before Lois seemed aware of her presence. Suddenly, she looked up and uttered a little cry, shrinking away from the dark figure. Then, as if her cry had loosened Grace's tongue, she began--

'Lois Barclay, did I ever do you any harm?' Grace did not know how often her want of loving-kindness had pierced the tender heart of the stranger under her roof; nor did Lois remember it against her now. Instead, Lois's memory was filled with grateful thoughts of how much that might have been left undone, by a less conscientious person, her aunt had done for her; and she half-stretched out her arms as to a friend in that desolate place, while she answered--

'Oh no, no! you were very good! very kind!'

But Grace stood immovable.

'I did you no harm, although I never rightly knew why you came to us.'

'I was sent by my mother on her death-bed,' moaned Lois, covering her face. It grew darker every instant. Her aunt stood, still and silent.

'Did any of mine every wrong you?' she asked, after a time.

'No, no; never, till Prudence said--Oh, aunt, do you think I am a witch?' And now Lois was standing up, holding by Grace's cloak, and trying to read her face. Grace drew herself, ever so little, away from the girl, whom she dreaded, and yet sought to propitiate.

'Wiser than I, godlier than I, have said it. But, oh, Lois, Lois! he was my first-born. Loose him from the demon, for the sake of Him whose name I dare not name in this terrible building, filled with them who have renounced the hopes of their baptism; loose Manasseh from his awful state, if ever I or mine did you a kindness.'

'You ask me for Christ's sake,' said Lois, 'I can name that holy name--for oh, aunt! indeed, and in holy truth, I am no witch! and yet I am to die--to be hanged! Aunt, do not let them kill me! I am so young, and I never did any one any harm that I know of.'

'Hush! for very shame! This afternoon I have bound my first-born with strong cords, to keep him from doing himself or us a mischief--he is so frenzied. Lois Barclay, look here!' and Grace knelt down at her niece's feet, and joined her hands, as if in prayer. 'I am a proud woman, God forgive me! and I never thought to kneel to any save to Him. And now I kneel at your feet, to pray you to release my children, more especially my son Manasseh, from the spells you have put upon them. Lois, hearken to me, and I will pray to the Almighty for you, if yet there may be mercy.'

I cannot do it; I never did you or yours any wrong. How can I undo it? How can I?' And she wrung her hands, in intensity of conviction of the inutility of aught she could do.

Here Grace got up, slowly, stiffly, and sternly. She stood aloof from the chained girl, in the remote corner of the prison-cell near the door, ready to make her escape as soon as she had cursed the witch, who would not, or could not, undo the evil she had wrought. Grace lifted up her right hand, and held it up on high, as she doomed Lois to be accursed for ever, for her deadly sin, and her want of mercy even at this final hour. And, lastly, she summoned her to meet her at the judgment-seat, and answer for this deadly injury, done to both souls and bodies of those who had taken her in, and received her when she came to them an orphan and a stranger.

Until this last summons, Lois had stood as one who hears her sentence and can say nothing against it, for she knows all would be in vain. But she raised her head when she heard her aunt speak of the judgment- seat, and at the end of Grace's speech she, too, lifted up her right hand, as if solemnly pledging herself by that action, and replied--

'Aunt! I will meet you there. And there you will know my innocence of this deadly thing. God have mercy on you and yours!'

Her calm voice maddened Grace; and, making a gesture as if she plucked up a handful of dust off the floor and threw it at Lois, she cried--

'Witch! witch! ask mercy for thyself--I need not your prayers. Witches' prayers are read backwards. I spit at thee, and defy thee!' And so she went away.

Lois sat moaning that whole night through. 'God comfort me! God strengthen me!' was all she could remember to say. She just felt that want, nothing more-- all other fears and wants seemed dead within her. And, when the gaoler brought in her breakfast the next morning, he reported her as 'gone silly'; for, indeed, she did not seem to know him, but kept rocking herself to and fro, and whispering softly to herself, smiling a little from time to time.

But God did comfort her, and strengthen her too. Late on that Wednesday afternoon they thrust another 'witch' into her cell, bidding the two, with opprobrious words, keep company together. The new-comer fell prostrate with the push given her from without; and Lois, not recognising any thing but an old ragged woman, lying helpless on her face on the ground, lifted her up; and lo! it was Nattee--dirty, filthy indeed, mud-pelted, stone-bruised, beaten, and all astray in her wits with the treatment she had received from the mob outside. Lois held her in her arms, and softly wiped the old brown wrinkled face with her apron, crying over it, as she had hardly yet cried over her own sorrows. For hours she tended the old Indian woman--tended her bodily woes; and, as the poor scattered senses of the savage creature came slowly back, Lois gathered her infinite dread of the morrow, when she, too, as well as Lois, was to be led out to die, in face of all that infuriated crowd. Lois sought in her own mind for some source of comfort for the old woman, who shook like one in the shaking-palsy at the dread of death--and such a death!

When all was quiet through the prison, in the deep dead midnight, the gaoler outside the door heard Lois telling, as if to a young child, the marvellous and sorrowful story of One who died on the cross for us and for our sakes. As long as she spoke, the Indian woman's terror seemed lulled; but, the instant she paused for weariness, Nattee cried out afresh, as if some wild beast were following her close through the 'dense forests in which she had dwelt in her youth. And then Lois went on, saying all the blessed words she could remember, and comforting the helpless Indian woman with the sense of the presence of a Heavenly Friend. And, in comforting her, Lois was comforted; in strengthening her, Lois was strengthened.

The morning came, and the summons to come forth and die came. They who entered the cell found Lois asleep, her face resting on the slumbering old woman, whose head she still held in her lap. She did not seem clearly to recognise where she was, when she awakened; the 'silly' look had returned to her wan face; all she appeared to know was that, somehow or another, through some peril or another, she had to protect the poor Indian woman. She smiled faintly, when she saw the bright light of the April day; and put her arm round Nattee, and tried to keep the Indian quiet with hushing, soothing words of broken meaning, and holy fragments of the Psalms. Nattee tightened her hold upon Lois, as they drew near the gallows, and the outrageous crowd below began to hoot and yell. Lois redoubled her efforts to calm and encourage Nattee, apparently unconscious that any of the opprobrium, the hootings, the stones, the mud, was directed towards herself. But, when they took Nattee from her arms, and led her out to suffer first, Lois seemed all at once to recover her sense of the present terror. She gazed wildly around, stretched out her arms as if to some person in the distance, who was yet visible to her, and cried out once, with a voice that thrilled through all who heard it, 'Mother!' Directly afterwards, the body of Lois the Witch swung in the air; and every one stood with hushed breath, with a sudden wonder, like a fear of deadly crime, fallen upon them.

The stillness and the silence were broken by one crazed and mad, who came rushing up the steps of the ladder, and caught Lois's body in his arms, and kissed her lips with wild passion. And then, as if it were true what the people believed, that he was possessed by a demon, he sprang down, and rushed through the crowd, out of the bounds of the city, and into the dark dense forest; and Manasseh Hickson was no more seen of Christian man.

The people of Salem had awakened from their frightful delusion before the autumn, when Captain Holdernesse and Hugh Lucy came to find out Lois, and bring her home to peaceful Barford, in the pleasant country of England. Instead, they led them to the grassy grave where she lay at rest, done to death by mistaken men. Hugh Lucy shook die dust off his feet in quitting Salem, with a heavy, heavy heart, and lived a bachelor all his life long for her sake.

Long years afterwards, Captain Holdernesse sought him out, to tell him some news that he thought might interest the grave miller of the Avon- side. Captain

Holdernesse told him, that in the previous year--it was then 1713--the sentence of excommunication against the witches of Salem was ordered, in godly sacramental meeting of the church, to be erased and blotted out, and that those who met together for this purpose 'humbly requested the merciful God would pardon whatsoever sin, error, or mistake was in the application of justice, through our merciful High Priest, who knoweth how to have compassion on the ignorant, and those that are out of the way.' He also said, that Prudence Hickson--now woman grown--had made a most touching and pungent declaration of sorrow and repentance before the whole church, for the false and mistaken testimony she had given in several instances, among which she particularly mentioned that of her cousin Lois Barclay. To all of which Hugh Lucy only answered--

'No repentance of theirs can bring her back to life.'

Then Captain Holdernesse took out a paper and read the following humble and solemn declaration of regret on the part of those who signed it, among whom Grace Hickson was one:--

'We, whose names are undersigned, being, in the year 1692, called to serve as jurors in the court of Salem, on trial of many who were by some suspected guilty of doing acts of witchcraft upon the bodies of sundry persons: we confess that we ourselves were not capable to understand, nor able to withstand, the mysterious delusions of the powers of darkness, and prince of the air, but were, for want of knowledge in ourselves, and better information from others, prevailed with to take up with such evidence against the accused, as, on further consideration, and better information, we justly fear was insufficient for the touching the lives of any (Deut. xvii. 6), whereby we feel we have been instrumental, with others, though ignorantly and unwittingly, to bring upon ourselves and this people of the Lord the guilt of innocent blood; which sin, the Lord saith in Scripture, he would not pardon (2 Kings xxiv. 4), that is, we suppose, in regard of his temporal judgments. We do, therefore, signify to all in general (and to the surviving sufferers in special) our deep sense of, and sorrow for, our errors, in acting on such evidence to the condemning of any person; and do hereby declare, that we justly fear that we were sadly deluded and mistaken, for which we are much disquieted and distressed in our minds, and do therefore humbly beg forgiveness, first of God for Christ's sake, for this our error; and pray that God would not impute the guilt of it to ourselves nor others; and we also pray that we may be considered candidly and aright by the living sufferers, as being then under the power of a strong and general delusion, utterly unacquainted with, and not experienced in, matters of that nature.

'We do heartily ask forgiveness of you all, whom we have justly offended; and do declare, according to our present minds, we would none of us do such things again on such grounds for the whole world; praying you to accept of this in way of satisfaction for our offence, and that you would bless the inheritance of the Lord, that he may be entreated for the land.

'Foreman, THOMAS FISK, c.'

To the reading of this paper Hugh Lucy made no reply save this, even more gloomily than before--

'All their repentance will avail nothing to my Lois, nor will it bring back her life.'

Then Captain Holdernesse spoke once more, and said that on the day of the general fast, appointed to be held all through New England, when the meeting-houses were crowded, an old, old man, with white hair, had stood up in the place in which he was accustomed to worship, and had handed up into the pulpit a written confession, which he had once or twice essayed to read for himself, acknowledging his great and grievous error in the matter of the witches of Salem, and praying for the forgiveness of God and of His people, ending with an entreaty that all then present would join with him in prayer that his past conduct might not bring down the displeasure of the Most High upon his country, his family, or himself That old man, who was no other than justice Sewall, remained standing all the time that his confession was read; and at the end he said, 'The good and gracious God be pleased to save New England and me and my family!' And then it came out that, for years past, judge Sewall had set apart a day for humiliation and prayer, to keep fresh in his mind a sense of repentance and sorrow for the part he had borne in these trials, and that this solemn anniversary he was pledged to keep as long as he lived, to show his feeling of deep humiliation.

Hugh Lucy's voice trembled as he spoke: 'All this will not bring my Lois to life again, or give me back the hope of my youth.'

But--as Captain Holdernesse shook his head (for what word could he say, or how dispute what was so evidently true?)--Hugh added, 'What is the day, know you, that this justice has set apart?'

'The twenty-ninth of April.'

'Then, on that day, will I, here at Barford in England, join my prayers as long as I live with the repentant judge, that his sin may be blotted out and no more had in remembrance. She would have willed it so.'

Made in the USA
Coppell, TX
22 January 2021

48532154R00056